Still
STANDING

ALSO BY COLLEEN COLEMAN

Don't Stop Me Now

I'm Still Standing

COLLEEN COLEMAN

Bookouture

Published by Bookouture
An imprint of StoryFire Ltd.
Carmelite House, 50 Victoria Embankment,
London, EC4Y 0DZ
United Kingdom
www.bookouture.com

ISBN: 978-1-78681-252-0
ISBN: 978-1-78681-395-4
eBook ISBN: 978-1-78681-251-3

This book is a work of fiction. Names, characters, businesses,
organizations, places and events other than those clearly in the
public domain, are either the product of the author's imagination
or are used fictitiously. Any resemblance to actual persons, living or
dead, events or locales is entirely coincidental.

To Elizabeth and Lorcan

For encouraging my sister and me to keep
our ideas high and bright

To keep working hard with our faces tilted skyward

To follow our dreams and reach for those stars

Always xxx

CHAPTER ONE

'Mr and Mrs O'Connor?'

'I'm Evelyn.' I shake the relationship counsellor's hand. 'I made the appointment.'

She nods, violet eyes piercing mine. 'Shannon Brannigan, very pleased to meet you. I must say, you two are the youngest couple we've ever had in here. Newly-weds?'

I shake my head. If only. We were all over each other when we were newly-weds. Inseparable. Couldn't keep our eyes or hands off each other. That all feels like a very long time ago now.

'No.' I shake my head. 'Married seven years, together ten.'

'Ah, I see. High-school sweethearts.'

We never dreamed we'd ever be somewhere like here, top floor in a plush city office block miles away from our cottage by the sea. We'd have scoffed at the idea. Counselling? Us? For God's sake. A complete waste of time and money. Touchy-feely claptrap. Too invasive. Too American. Too expensive. Our attitude would have been that if you need to come to relationship counselling, then you need to break up. Simple as that. *Our attitude.* I check that. This is still James's attitude now. I know he thinks coming here is a stupid idea. We used to be united in our thoughts and dreams and attitudes.

Not now.

Not for a long time now.

Shannon Brannigan holds out her hand to James. I can tell by his bored, glazed look that he's not been listening, just staring at her stock beach-scene screen saver – sun, sea and surf. Typical.

I nudge him.

He scowls at me like I'm his mum and he's a hassled teenager. Honestly, the kids I teach are more mature.

He shakes her hand and offers a half-hearted smile. I had to drag him here, and he actually looks like he has been dragged. Long, unruly curls in a knotty blonde Afro, basketball vest and sunglasses. Indoors. Ray-Bans in cloudy, drizzly Irish weather. I ask you. Reality check, James. We're not in Ibiza now. I actually just avert my eyes. Effort? Personal pride? Basic manners? I'm not going there. It gives me a headache.

'What?' he says.

I say nothing. Look to the screen saver too. White sand, turquoise sea. Looks like one of our honeymoon photos. That time now feels like it belonged to somebody else. To my left, I can feel James surveying me.

'Just because you dress like a politician. There's no dress code, right?'

I'm in my work clothes. Because I've come straight from my grown-up, responsible job that requires me to not play FIFA till the early hours every night of the week, to get up and be ready on time and wear actual clean professional clothes that were purchased this decade and not scraped off the carpet with my foot after pressing snooze twenty times. If I could rewind and meet James now, for the first time, would I even give him a second glance? Possibly not. He's good-looking, no doubt about that, but I'd think, nah, too cool, too affected; not my type. And if for some weird reason we ended up on a date, I just know I'd pick up on the warning signs. I'd speed-read his laziness, his selfishness, his sarcasm and his intolerable messiness. And I'd say: I'm out. I'd run. I'd run a MILE.

Shannon Brannigan claps her hands together. 'Follow me, you two, this way.' She seems a bit smug, like she's seen it all before. She's probably thinking: *Settled down too quick. Grew up and grew apart.*

I hope not, though. I'd like to think she'll come up with something a bit less clichéd for her extortionate fee. Maybe she'll give us a series of date nights to complete to rekindle our love, or recommend some tantric titbits that will elevate us to a new level of intimacy and therefore make us stop eye-rolling every time the other speaks. And if so, that makes this incredibly straightforward. Maybe I've just counselled us to a resolution before even sinking into her sofa of a million cushions. James and I got married too soon to know who we really were, and now, seven years later, we have grown into two completely different people. But these things happen to couples all the time, and she'll write us a bespoke marriage prescription that will see us shipshape and tickety-boo in no time. Yeah, that makes the colossal fee sound like good value after all.

Ms Brannigan offers us two seats side by side and James rolls his eyes and sticks his hands deep into his jeans. I really hope she knows what she's doing. Hope she has that marriage prescription ready, because we can't go on as we are or we'll kill each other.

'Can I get you a drink? Take a moment to orient yourself with your surroundings.'

James finds the window and stares at it like he's planning to jump through it.

She pours us some water. 'How did you find me?' she asks.

'Online.' I take a sip and elbow James. We're here, we're paying; for God's sake act like you are bothered. I decide not to tell her that she was just a pop-up ad that got into my brain after my daily Google search of *Is the seven-year itch real? How do you know if you should stay married? How many young marriages survive? Why is my husband such an idiot? Does it ever get better... really?*

I thought maybe I could just become more understanding and accepting of James, let things go, stop caring so much, but it's impossible. And yes, I get that he hasn't cheated on me (too lazy), or tried to push me down the stairs (not up early enough), or emptied our bank account (can't remember his PIN… ever). So there's no big stuff, but there's an awful lot of small stuff. A constant, relentless, teeming downpour of infuriating, exhausting, draining, arse-aching small stuff. And I can't see the good amongst it any more.

'I've studied your pre-session questionnaires.'

'Questionnaires? More like an interrogation. There were nearly one hundred questions on that thing,' says James.

Inwardly I sigh with relief that he actually completed it. At least she has something to work with. At least it shows a little bit of willing on his part.

'Thank you, I appreciate your co-operation. They were very insightful and really helped to inform me about where you two are at right now – as a couple and as individuals. The very fact that you are both here today is a real positive. It means that you are ready to change for the better, whatever it takes. I want to help you overcome any perceived obstacles and get you back on track.'

That's true, I really do want change. I want to mow down any perceived obstacles and leap into something new, something meaningful and happy and fulfilling. I straighten up in my seat. James pulls his hands down his face and blows out his cheeks.

'Try to be honest at all times. Remember, this is a safe place. I'm not here to judge you. I have no agenda other than to help you realise what the best course of action is. I believe that you already know what you need to do, that you already know the nature of the problem, and deep down you know the right solution. I'm here to help you find your own way to that solution. Sound okay?'

We both nod. Solutions. That's what we're here for.

'I thought we'd start with a little game. Just an ice-breaker to get us talking, to open up some new lines of communication. Explore areas we may have neglected until now.'

She reaches under the table and pulls out a board game that looks similar to Monopoly.

'Let's dive straight in. I find this game an excellent tool, particularly for couples who appear locked into the same narrative. James, please roll the dice, then move your counter, and whatever colour space you land on, please select a card of that colour.'

James shifts forwards in his chair, picking up the dice without making eye contact with either of us and breathing heavily through his nose. He rolls a six, moves to a red square and selects a red TRUTH card, which reads: *Describe your partner.*

'Past or present?' he asks.

The cheek! I turn around to challenge. 'What's that supposed to mean?'

Shannon rests a hand on my knee. 'The other player must remain silent and allow the speaker an uninterrupted opportunity to respond.'

James cracks his first smile of the day. 'Uninterrupted? Silent? Now we're getting somewhere.' He rubs his hands together. 'Past: my partner was happy. Present: she's unhappy. *Very* unhappy. Very snappy. All the time.'

I squirm in my seat. 'Um… that's not true. I am happy sometimes, just not often around you.' The words are out before I realise it. Shannon holds a finger to her lips. 'Sorry,' I whisper into my chest.

James continues. 'She used to listen, but now she doesn't. She used to do other stuff rather than just work all the time and then come home and bitch about work and then fall asleep on the couch because she's tired from work and then spend time calling people from work to talk about work some more. We used to do stuff together. Nice stuff. We used to be happy. She used to laugh and joke around, but now she just moans and sighs and sometimes shouts and yells.' He flicks me a look. 'I'm just saying how it is, Evelyn.'

I need to sit on my hands to steady them, I'm that angry. This marriage counselling was supposed to be about James realising he was a crappy husband; this is not about me. I nag and snap and yell because he makes me do it! If he just did what he was supposed to, when he was supposed to, and to a decent standard, I'd not have to go on at him like I do. My face is flushed with infuriation. I need to get myself together. I can't sit here with a red face and fit to claw his eyes out and then claim I'm not bad-tempered. I take a big gulp of water and steady myself.

'Thank you for your truth.' Shannon nods to James. 'Evelyn, it's your turn. Roll the dice whenever you're ready.'

Slowly I shake the dice with all the apprehension of a gambler with everything to lose. I roll a two. Purple space. I take a purple WISH card and read it aloud.

'If you woke up in the morning and everything amiss in your life had disappeared, what would your day be like?'

Oh wow. I like this wish card. I wish it was more than a wish. An image springs to mind immediately. I can envisage it like a beautiful movie.

'I'd wake up fully rested. I'd open my eyes and it would be so peaceful. The house would be clean, uncluttered, almost fragrant. There'd be no crap anywhere, no need to nag or argue, no sarcastic comments. I'd go to work and I'd have the energy to do my job really well because I was happy and relaxed, and when I got home, I'd call my girlfriends. We might go out to the theatre or go shopping, share a bottle of wine in town. I'd get back to a nice ordered house, my favourite music playing lightly in the background, and look forward to a bath and a book and slipping into bed, then doing it all over again the next day.'

'Is that it?' asks James. 'If you could do anything you wanted, you'd work and have a bath in a tidy house?' Eye roll.

'Yeah, it is. Quite a simple existence, I suppose. I'm actually quite calmed by the thought of it,' I tell Shannon. 'Bliss. Order. Peacefulness.'

'James, if you drew that card, how would you have responded?' she asks.

He stretches back into his seat, smiling. 'I'd wake up in a beachfront villa, sun in the sky. I'm all by myself, no work, no responsibility, no lists of jobs, no emails from banks and insurers and tax bullshit. Nobody telling me what to do or how to do it. No one judging or criticising, nagging me… just me and the sun and the sand between my toes.' His cheeks are flushed, and there's an animation in his eyes I haven't seen for a long time.

'And an ice-cold pitcher of mojito?' I venture.

He smiles and rubs his hands down his thighs, nodding. 'Oh yes.'

Shannon lets the silence settle between us. 'Two very different ideas of what a dream life would look like. And that's perfectly fine; usually that's not a problem, usually it's something we can work with.'

Usually? We both shift up slightly, lean in to hear what she has to say.

'But the issue I'm having with you two is that I'm not convinced you actually want to go forward – either of you, as a married couple.'

'Pardon me?' I ask, confused.

I can tell James is slightly confused too. He tilts his head to listen more carefully, his fingers stroking his stubbly chin. 'What do you mean exactly?'

'I don't think either of you really wants to be married any more,' she says matter-of-factly. Like it's obvious.

I'm shaking my head at her, and then at James. I thought she was supposed to fix us up. I thought her job was to write the marriage prescription. The eye-wateringly costly tantric marriage prescription.

'I'm sorry, but I'm just not following,' I tell her. James shushes me and leans forward, elbows on his knees.

'My deep concern is that neither of you included the other in your vision. Not once. Not in any way. If anything, you became most at ease and hopeful at the thought of being apart, at having a space, at feeling free to live your lives as your best selves – and you have very definite and different ideas about what that looks like.' She focuses on me, violet eyes, wide and earnest.

'Evelyn, does any part of you share James's vision?'

I bite down on my lip. I can't lie. She'll know. He'll know. I'll know. 'Before, in the past maybe... but not now.'

I look into my plastic cup. No more water.

'James, does any part of you share Evelyn's vision?'

He taps his lips thoughtfully. 'No.' He makes eye contact with me for the first time since we entered this office. 'And Evelyn, I'm sorry to say this, but I don't think I ever will.'

We stew in our confessions, the silence between us growing thick and hot. I guess it would make sense for us to argue now. For me to tell him why it is completely impractical and impossible for him to just turn his back on his construction business, for us to leave our family and friends and all responsibility to go and live like complete hedonists somewhere on the Balearic coast.

But I don't say a word. I feel like we've already said everything. I wait for him to speak, to try and convince me. But he doesn't. Maybe this is the first thing we've actually agreed on in ages.

Shannon hands us each a mini whiteboard and a chunky black marker.

'We've considered your desires, your innermost dreams about what would bring you happiness. Now I want us to consider the future. It's really important that you answer honestly, without influence from peers or parents or each other.'

I swallow hard. That's not easy. I've never made a decision without influence from peers or parents or James. I'm glad it's a wipeable board – something about being able to erase this instantly without trace lessens my anxiety about what she's going to ask me to do. *Us* to do. We are still in this together. We may still be able to work things out. Maybe all that earlier was just a scare tactic, pretending that we're unfixable, that our marriage is over and we need to split. What would people think? The shame of it. It would be easier to stay together just to avoid being village gossip, I think. But I guess that's why we're here. Because we're not finding staying together easy at all.

I take the lid off my marker.

'If all your dreams came true, how would you like to see yourself in five years' time? What's your life like? What have you achieved? What are you proud of?' She nods to signal that we should begin.

At first I dare not write anything. It's too precious, too personal. What if they shake their heads or pull a face or ask me for details as to how exactly I'm going to get from here to there in my perfect world? I don't want to write down anything that they might disprove or rationalise out of existence.

I'm not pausing because I don't know. I've got a crystal-clear idea of what I want, but I don't know if I'm ready to share it yet. I doodle a moment on my board, then rub it out with my sleeve. I'm really not sure about this. It's a lot to put out there. And at the moment, it feels very fragile. It can hardly hold its own weight in terms of possibility.

I look over to James; he's still staring out of the window.

'Take your time,' says Shannon. 'We can take as much time as you need.'

With that, James straightens up in his seat and starts writing on his board with intense focus.

Okay, if James is getting stuck in, then I need to pull my finger out. I twirl my marker in my fingers, close my eyes and try to imagine my life in five years. I'll be thirty-three. I see it in my mind's eye, clear as day. It's like I'm watching a snippet of a home movie with a cast of characters from my life, but we are all on set in some unknown location. We're at a party, and I'm wearing a huge maternity dress. My mother is nearby, laughing with my sister, and there are lots and lots of happy, smiling people around – eating, drinking, dancing. I'm perfectly happy, I'm the happiest I've ever been, and I rub my swollen tummy, so excited about the future, about this forever family.

But how realistic is this? Every time I've brought it up with James, that maybe I should come off the pill, that we could start trying for a baby, he rubs his neck and sighs and says that we agreed we wouldn't do that until we finish the cottage properly, until we turn thirty, until we go on another holiday, until he finishes his latest job. There's always something else to do first, always waiting until…

'Ready?' asks Shannon. I am jolted from my thoughts. I scribble down two bullet points.

- To start a family (1–4 children, but happy with whatever, don't want to sound greedy)
- Cottage to be finished

I reimagine my party scene and realise how important this is to me. In five years' time I want to be living a life of purpose, full of hope and love and meaning. I want my life to feel like it's begun, rather than shuffling around aimlessly in a waiting room located somewhere between the past and the future. Seven years ago, we bought our dream house, a seaside cottage in our home town, on a hill overlooking the Atlantic. It was near derelict, but that made it affordable. And after all, I wanted to put our own stamp on it, develop its potential. With James being a builder, you'd imagine that it would be straightforward. Except the last thing he feels like doing after a day's work is more building. Hence we have an unfinished construction-site shell of a house. So my dream in five years? To have a home worth inviting people into, a space filled with laughter and music. Friends and family could come to stay – a guest room for my sister when she comes down from Dublin, even my mother when she babysits! Oh, and a nursery…

I look over at James. He finishes writing and places his marker on the table with a satisfied grin.

Shannon opens her hands towards us both. 'Show each other your boards, please.'

Right, here goes everything.

James squints at mine. 'Children and house, basically. No surprises there.'

I nod. 'This isn't a game, James. I didn't come here to trick you.'

I lean in to read his. It looks like a long equation.

$$5 \text{ years} = 260 \text{ weeks}$$
$$260 \text{ weeks} = 1,820 \text{ days}$$
$$1,820 \text{ days} = 43,680 \text{ hours}$$
$$43,680 \text{ hours} = 2,620,800 \text{ minutes}$$

'Do I know what I am doing in 2,620,800 minutes time?' he says. 'No, I don't. I think it's fairly ridiculous looking that far ahead yet.'

Even Shannon inhales deeply.

James shrugs. 'I don't get why this is a big deal. Who knows what could happen between now and then? We might be completely different people, wanting totally different things. That happened before, so why wouldn't it happen again? It's a useless activity. Simple as that.'

And it is as simple but also as complex as that. This is the moment when it becomes clear that staying together is holding us both back. For better or for worse, it is time to go our separate ways. Although we can't get on, we love and respect each other too much to keep throwing all our energy into fixing something that is unfixable. We were the first of all our friends to fall in love, the first to promise forever, and now we're the first to realise that we've made a massive boob. The end of the road for Mr and Mrs O'Connor, and back to being Evelyn Dooley.

But this time I'm a twenty-eight-year-old divorcee without the faintest idea about what's supposed to happen next.

After we thank Shannon Brannigan for her help, James and I take the lift together down to the ground-floor reception. We stare ahead at the brushed-metal doors, both in shock, unsure of what is supposed to happen next. Incredulous at everything we've learnt in such a short time, stunned that such a momentous decision took less time than a trip to IKEA.

'Are we really going to go through with this?' I ask.

James takes a deep breath. 'I guess so. Time for a new chapter. What do you think?'

'It's going to be weird at first, for a while. But I agree, new chapter.' I nudge him with my elbow. 'Just think, no more driving at the speed limit. No more poncey wine. No more having to sit through *MasterChef*. Plenty to look forward to.' I smile.

He smiles too, and nudges me back. 'You've got a point there. And what about you? No more speeding tickets, or boxers left on the stairs, or cigarette butts by the back door.'

The lift doors open. But we don't leave; instead, I turn to him.

'We weren't all bad, Mr O'Connor. We had some good times.'

He nods, his eyes meeting mine. 'Good luck, Evelyn. I mean it. I hope everything works out.'

'You too.'

We hug our final goodbyes, then step out of the lift and go our separate ways. Choosing to go it alone, to walk into the life that awaits us, whatever it may hold.

I cross the street, climb into my car and start to drive. I don't head in any particular direction; I just want to hit the road, to feel like I'm going somewhere. I turn on the radio, shake out my hair and roll down the windows.

Wow. It's done. And we're both okay.

In fact I think we're both a bit excited.

I put my foot down on the accelerator and turn up the music. I know I am.

CHAPTER TWO

Three months later

Bacon. The most effective alarm clock in the world. I can hear it sizzling. Despite myself, I can feel my body gravitating towards it like a homing device. The smell of oak-smoked rashers fried in butter wafts down the hall and curls into my bedroom.

I am back home. I can tell before I even open my eyes – the glorious aroma of a full Irish on the go, the whistling of the kettle on the Aga, the lowing of cattle out the back, the local radio station announcing updated hourly news on weather and funeral arrangements.

I cup my hands over my eyes. I've slept so much while I've been here. Mum reckons I must have needed it. Emotional burnout or adrenal fatigue or just being knackered and needing some good old-fashioned Mammy Dooley cosseting and lots of rest. Whatever it is, I do feel better. Only problem is, it's almost like I never left. And that's not a good sign for a fully grown woman. I'll have to get my own place, learn to live on my own, start thinking about the specifics of that… but not just yet. Before I came here, I was too stressed to think about it. Now I'm probably too relaxed to hassle myself with a task that I can simply put off for another day.

So here I am, back at the farmhouse. Tucked into the bottom bunk, which is still covered in stickers of fairies and love hearts alongside the encrypted initials of crushes we had through our teenage years, etched into the metal frame. I'm back, on the other side of love's young dream, in the bedroom I shared with my sister all my pre-marriage life.

'Evelyn, are you up? Breakfast is on the table.'

I know it's lovely that she's mothering me. *Smothering* me in lovingly buttered slices of home-made bread and cheese and freshly laid hen's eggs and lashings of milky sugared tea... But I can't go on like this. I know it myself: for my own self-respect and cholesterol count, I need to start thinking of moving out... again.

'Did you hear me, Evelyn? Get it while it's hot.'

I groan and kick off the duvet and can't help but think that I was probably a bit hasty in moving out of the cottage. Yes, it is the site of my heartache, yes, it's a health-and-safety nightmare, but at least it didn't make me feel nine years old again.

I make my way to the kitchen wearing huge bear-paw slippers, and stand in the doorway in my dressing gown, rubbing my eyes in the morning sunlight.

'Sit down there and get that inside you. Great way to start the day.' She adds another sausage to my plate. And then a slice of black pudding.

'Mum, please, I can't keep eating like this.'

She looks up at me. 'What's wrong with... Oh my word, hold on.'

She dashes back to the Aga, tea towel ready in her hand, and comes back with a bowl of wild mushrooms.

'That's the job.' She sits, smiling to herself. 'Now, what could possibly be wrong with that? Great feed, fit for a king.'

'It is. It's delicious. But I'm going to be the size of a house.' And this is just breakfast. Elevenses will be a hot-out-of-the-oven slice of her moist tea-soaked fruit cake with home-made blackberry jam. Lunch will be a huge plate of fresh salad and herbs from the garden with honey-glazed ham, and dinner will be... Oh, I'm ready to burst at the thought of it. Beef and Guinness pie with creamy mash, or Irish stew with dumplings, or corned beef and cabbage… Anything that comes in at less than ten thousand calories a portion is considered a snack.

'So this is it for today, Mum, okay? I need to cut back,' I tell her as I bite into a slice of her home-baked soda bread. God, this is good. I'll start the diet after breakfast. No point starting now, not when it's so fresh and warm.

She regards me a minute, grinds salt and pepper over the mushrooms and shoves the bowl across the table to me.

'There isn't a mother in the country that likes seeing her daughter pale and skinny. You've colour coming back into those cheeks now and you've gained a bit of weight. No harm. No harm at all.' She raises her fork in the air. 'Eat that up now! Think of all the poor starving children in the world who haven't a bite, and you with a big plate in front of you!'

I help myself to a heaped spoonful of mushrooms. Any previous plan to studiously push whatever food I don't want around on my plate evaporates very quickly when my mother pulls this little guilt trip. There's little chance of getting one over on her. She knows what works. Every time.

This isn't exactly how I imagined things would be post-break-up. I was right when I told James that it would be weird at first. It still is. You get so used to someone that not seeing them every day feels like you are on holiday. It doesn't feel as though it's going to be like this forever. We didn't choose a two-week break from one another – we chose to untangle our lives entirely, pack our bags and buy one-way tickets out. And that takes a while to sink in.

Once the initial admin and logistics of packing and sorting and shifting everything from bank accounts to bedding was done, I felt that the easiest thing was to move back in with my mother. We both felt it was better to make a clean break, too hard to stay amongst all the reminders of an unrealised dream. James decided he was going to take some time off, go travelling. I spent every spare hour I had painting walls, planting the garden, varnishing floors and surfaces to try and add value to the cottage, to try and make it as saleable as possible. Once it was empty and in good nick we could put it on the market immediately. The farmhouse that I grew up in has plenty of room for me to store all my boxes, and my bedroom is virtually untouched since I left, so it seemed like a very natural and sensible choice at the time. But now that I've been here a while, I realise that this can't be a permanent situation if I really want to get out there and do something with my life and my new-found freedom.

At first I loved being spoilt and mollycoddled. I haven't lifted a finger since moving in here; Mum does all the laundry, cooking and housework. It's bliss in that way. But I have to stop myself from getting too comfortable, because if I stay like this, I'll never accomplish anything; Mum will just do it for me, wanting to save me the trouble, stepping in so I don't even have to break a sweat. Now that the legal stuff has settled down and I've had time to adjust to moving out of the cottage and not being James's wife any more, I'm going to have to re-enter the real world.

I guess it's natural to want to hide away after a major life change; you need time to think, to work out your next move. It all boils down to self-protection. Mum taking care of all the day-to-day stuff has really given me space and time to think without distraction. Time to think about what I really want from my life. So far, I've just discovered what I *don't* want; I don't want to build my life around someone else ever again. But that's as far as I've got. Whatever move I make next, I want to be absolutely sure that it's the right one. I'm hoping I'll recognise that move when I see it.

By the time it's dark outside, I'm chatting to my sister on Skype.

'This is an OPPORTUNITY, Evelyn,' declares Tara, sipping white wine in her LAX hotel room. Given the eight-hour time difference, it's an early tipple, but as an air stewardess, Tara doesn't mark the passage of time in day and night, light and dark. Only in terms of departure and arrival, work time and playtime. 'This could turn out to be the biggest, most important opportunity of your life!'

On hearing this, my mother inhales sharply and brings her hand down on the kitchen table behind me. 'What are you on about, Tara? Her marriage has failed. How in the name of God could that be considered an opportunity? It is a catastrophe, that's what it is. An utter disaster in every sense.'

She strides up behind me, fuming, and leans in over my shoulder so she's facing Tara on screen. 'Easy for you to say, missy. Gallivanting on the other side of the world. You're not here in the thick of things. You know what Ballybeg is like! Whispers and nudges and pointed questions. Only yesterday, I was grilled in the hairdresser's: "Is it true that your daughter and young James O'Connor have split up? Was he carrying on behind her back? Or was it her?" And you know who I spotted with her head in the sink the whole time? None other than Mrs O'Connor herself! Oh, the shame of it. I didn't know where to look. I've had no peace since this bloody "opportunity".'

We sit silently, Tara and me, thousands of miles apart, on either side of the Atlantic, both of us knowing better than to fan the flames or interrupt or, God forbid, disagree. Mum pulls her cardigan round her shoulders and swigs the last of her cardboard-coloured tea from a china cup.

'I'm taking the dog for a walk. I've had enough of listening to this nonsense. I don't know what planet you two are on. Why you can't just settle down and be happy is beyond me.'

Muffin rushes over to her, shuttling around her feet excitedly. Mum pulls on her wellingtons and grabs the dog's lead, raising her eyes to catch mine.

'You know what it is that confuses me, Evelyn? Did you honestly believe that every day of marriage was going to be kisses and roses?

I was married to your father for thirty years. Was every day love's young dream? Of course it wasn't. But that's life. You get up and you get on with it. It's still love. It's still marriage. But it's called sticking things out. And if you ask me, it wasn't love or friendship that was lacking between you and James – it was sticking power. Never mind that marriage counsellor, she only made things worse; you should have come to me. I would have sorted the two of you out.'

She shakes her head and mutters something to herself about Jesus, Mary and Joseph granting her strength. And patience. And sanity. Muffin grabs a ball in her mouth and runs to the door, her tail wagging.

'Come on, Muffin, let's get out into the fresh air and leave these two to their "opportunities".'

The door slams shut behind them and they are gone.

'Oh my God, she's livid,' says Tara from behind her glass.

'I know. Usually she's fine, but if she goes into town and meets her friends, that triggers it all again. Which is awkward now that I've moved back in.'

'What's happened to the cottage?'

'We're hoping for a quick sale. James left all the paperwork to me, told me he didn't care how much it went for as long as it was as painless as possible. So if we can actually find a buyer, I'll take the first reasonable offer that comes in. I invested nearly everything I had in that cottage, so until it's sold, I'm not free to take on anything new. I don't think I can stand being here much longer, though. It's all a bit tense. I thought Mum would mellow over the split, but she hasn't.'

Tara sloshes another generous pour into her glass.

'And where's James gone? Is he back with his folks too?'

'No, he's still travelling. He's probably halfway to Ibiza as we speak.'

'Or crashed out on a mate's floor having missed his flight, or fighting with security at the airport because he's lost his passport... James can't get from A to B without you.'

Out of habit, I go to twist my wedding ring. But it's not there. Of course it's not. It's boxed up in the garage along with my wedding dress, a decade's worth of photo albums and everything else that I thought was priceless but that now holds absolutely no value to me at all.

'How's work?' asks Tara.

'It's fine, same old St Mary's. I'll manage.'

'Evelyn? C'mon, spill the beans. Mum isn't around now, you can talk to me.'

'It's crap. Fionnuala got promoted ahead of me and O'Driscoll has it in for me. I know she'd love to see the back of me. If you're not playing happy families, you're a pariah in her book. She told me that she doesn't want to draw unnecessary attention to my personal affairs. That the bishop looks unfavourably on such things and that as far as she's concerned I'm a school ambassador therefore my name will stay as Mrs O'Connor for as long as I decide to stay at the school.'

'You have got to be kidding. That is ILLEGAL. She can't say that to you, she can't tell you what your name is…'

'Yeah, I know, but what am I supposed to do? Ring up my human-rights lawyer?'

'You need to get out of there.'

'I can't just leave.'

'Yes you can.'

'Sure, I'll think about it,' I lie. There's no way I really will. Things will settle down. Mum will soften, the town gossips will move on to somebody else soon enough, and work… well, I'll get used to it.

But Tara isn't finished with me yet. 'You need a change. A fresh start. You need to get away from everything and begin your life again.'

'That would look great: first I quit my marriage and then I quit my job… my full-time, permanent, pensionable, professional job…'

She puts down her glass and leans into the screen.

'Evelyn, I know you're scared. I know you've been hit a hard blow. But you've played it safe and sensible your entire life – local teacher, married the boy next door, bought a cottage in the village – and look where it's got you.'

'Oh thanks, Tara, I'm feeling loads better now.'

'No, what I'm saying is, there are no guarantees. You tried it the good-girl way; now try it your own way, do something just for you.'

She makes it all sound so easy. I have to admit, I love the idea of trying something new, some*where* new. But what? And where?

'What about Mum?'

'She's fine. She has a big group of friends and her own life to lead now. This is your time to find yourself. You're twenty-eight, not eighty-eight. Move up to Dublin and live with me. With these transatlantic flights, I'm away a lot of the time. My flat is small but we've got the space. Inez won't mind – in fact she'd love to meet you. I'm always telling her about you. And when I'm around, we can top and tail just like old times.'

I laugh at the idea. Dad built our bunk beds due to Tara's relentless badgering. Once they were built, she never lasted a whole night in her own bunk without swinging her head down and asking me to climb up and cuddle in beside her. I shake my head. Two grown women – a teacher and an air hostess – back to squeezing into a single shared bed. It feels like I've worked so hard climbing ladders only to slide back down to the first square on the board.

'You know what Dad would say.' She gives me a soft, considered look.

'Set your sights on the sky and reach for the stars,' we both say in unison.

She's right. My father didn't sweat the small stuff. He kept his eyes on the prize at all times. He wanted us to keep moving forward, keep pressing on towards our goals; if you fall on the way, he would say, ask for help, dust yourself off, try another route. I know he'd want me to start my journey again, not stand still too long. So much to see, so much to aim for.

There's a knock on Tara's hotel room door. 'Oops! Gotta go, heading out now. Think about what I said, okay? I love you. Let me help you. It's what we do, right?'

I nod and blow her a kiss goodbye, and then she's gone.

I sit at my mum's kitchen table. No sound but the ticking clock and a braying donkey in the field out back. Dublin. It does sound tempting. Getting on a train and leaving all this behind is really, really tempting. Imagine turning this page over, turning the page on my mother's obsession with village tittle-tattle, on Mrs O'Driscoll's dictatorship, on driving past the empty cottage looking sad and deserted with its big For Sale sign outside. I've just replaced a stifling situation with James with a suffocating situation with Mum. I love her, but we're not meant to be housemates at this stage in our lives. I need my own space; I need to rebuild my life. Returning to my pre-James life isn't the answer. This really could be an opportunity. This could be the opportunity I've been waiting for.

I bite the top of my thumbnail. Leaving is one thing, but what would I be going to? No money, no job, scabbing some floor space in my sister's flat. Is that really an opportunity? At least here I have a home, I have security. It's only Dublin, four hours' drive away, but moving from house to house, bed to bed is the easy bit. Anyone can pack a bag and exchange one set of keys for another. But I've got to be honest with myself: it's far more than that. And it's going to involve a lot more than throwing some essentials together and buying a train ticket. It takes courage, real courage, to walk away from one life, to say goodbye to everything you know, to leave the comfort of the familiar and the well-loved and begin again from scratch.

I walk over to the sink and gaze out into the sparkling sky. It is beautiful here. My mother can't understand why anyone would want to live anywhere else. Here our night sky is as dark as you will find anywhere, and our view of the stars is unparalleled. We live on the most remote edge of Europe. From here I can see where the land meets the sea and the sea meets the sky and the sky meets the land all over again, a fluid palette of green to white to blue in the daytime and star-studded inky black at night. It is a precious place, a magical place, and the only place I've ever lived. The rolling waves of the Atlantic crash day and night against our shores; have done for thousands of years. An unbroken action, an uninterrupted sound linking everything past to our present. Yet every day, the coastline changes, every minute it is shaken up and rearranged by the elements. And right now I feel like my life has to be completely shaken up and rearranged to help me find the one I'm meant to lead.

Set your sights on the sky and reach for the stars.

As children, every time we faced something that seemed insurmountable – from long division to cross-country races – we'd run down the lane to Dad, crying and kicking and insisting that we couldn't do it, we weren't ready for it yet. Too much, too hard, too impossible. And he'd tell us that the outcome was of no concern to him; it would take care of itself and be joyous as long as we were willing to begin. That was all we had to do: set our sights, start well and he would be proud of us.

Tara's right. He'd want me to begin to make my life again. Begin with tears in my eyes, pain in my heart, empty pockets and a broken past, but begin. Everything needs a beginning. And once you begin, who knows what adventure awaits? Reach for the stars and you'll land somewhere higher than you ever imagined.

I open my laptop, my finger hovering over the Facebook icon. I promised myself I wouldn't stalk James on social media. But right now, on the cusp of making another huge life change, I need to see how he's doing. How he's coping with everything being shaken up. I take a deep breath and quickly click it.

His image flashes up on the screen. Just two minutes ago, he posted a photo. He's sitting on a stool at a bamboo counter, the blazing orange horizon in the background. He's already looking tanned, relaxed, happy, a mojito in hand. His eyes look brighter, like he's been laughing. I study the photo more carefully and see new, unfamiliar chunky black markings on his forearm. The tattoo he's wanted for years. Something he wanted that I talked him out of. I look to his naked wedding finger. There's no tan line, no mark to say that this is out of the ordinary, that this is unusual.

This is the new normal. Me sitting at the kitchen table on a Saturday night wondering what life is happening elsewhere. Someone is typing in the comment box under his photo. *Living the dream, mate!* Our break-up has given my ex-husband wings. Whereas I feel as though mine have been clipped.

I hear my mother's footsteps and Muffin's panting as they approach the front door. 'Evelyn? Are you still here?'

Yes. Still here. Sitting alone in the kitchen of my childhood home in a ball of Primark fleece, afraid of what home truth my mother might deliver next.

Muffin scampers in ahead of her and rushes over to my knees, jumping up on me, eyes bright, full of unconditional love and enthusiasm. I stroke her head and nuzzle into her neck. She wags her tail and tries to talk to me in her cute whimpering way. Why can't everyone just be a bit more dog? Why can't we love like this all the time? Be with each other the way we are with non-humans?

I look Muffin in the eyes. 'Someday I'm going to be the person you think I am.'

The person Tara thinks I am. The person I want to be.

And then it strikes me who that person is. A flash, a glimpse, and right there and then I know what I've got to do. Before my mother has even shaken off her second wellie and set foot inside the kitchen, I've texted my sister.

Ready or not, Dublin here I come.

Because I've set my sights and it's time for me to reach for those stars.

CHAPTER THREE

I hoist my bags from the bus, dragging them through the busy city centre towards O'Connell Street, where hopefully I'll be able to flag a cab. The empty footpaths start to narrow and crowd with hurried office workers, aimless tourists, distracted shoppers. I cross the Ha'Penny Bridge and pass clusters of market traders selling everything from fresh flowers to charm bracelets. The city is beautiful: tall red-brick buildings with stained-glass windows; old-fashioned shop signs alongside light and airy modern cafés and restaurants full of smiling baristas and smelling of fresh coffee. The River Liffey is as still as glass, sparkling in the midday sunshine.

I turn the corner into the main shopping strip, the streets lined on either side with flyer distributors to further clog the pedestrian traffic. The crowd stalls to almost a standstill by the next bus stop. Yes, people of Dublin, please continue to walk as slowly as humanly possible as though it is you alone who exists in the world. And just when you think you are walking as slowly as possible, challenge yourself to go slower again, almost to the point of walking backwards into a little something I like to call my personal space. Or don't. Whatever. The woman in front of me stabs her umbrella into my toe and the man behind me coughs a speck of phlegm onto my neck.

Maybe this was a mistake.

Maybe I'm just not cut out to be in a city. Too loud, too packed, too dirty. Research could actually prove that the amount of time

I spend in crowded urban places negatively correlates with how much I care about the human race at this moment in time…

I look up and down the street, trying to spot a friendly face so that I can confirm the directions I've been given, but nobody smiles or makes eye contact with me. The traffic is chaotic and there's a definite city stench hanging in the air, but it's only to be expected that I'd notice that. After all, I've lived my entire life on the most staggeringly beautiful and remote edge of the Atlantic coast. We don't just breathe fresh air; it whips us in the face, it lifts us and carries us over rock and sand, the music of it whistling and whooshing around us constantly in the crashing waves and wild winds.

But here in Dublin, I can only hear sirens. And horns. And the shouts of angry drivers undercut by the frustrated mumbling outrage of cyclists and commuters. So many people getting in your way, in your space, under your feet. I've hardly covered any ground at all but I feel like I've crossed a minefield.

And there's something else here. Something unsettling. I can't help but notice the number of homeless people huddled under blankets by the bridge railings, their cupped hands held out in front of them. I place a few coins in each as I walk towards the cab rank. I know every capital city has its share of poverty and homelessness, but it shocks me to see it up close: so many people hurrying past so many other people sitting on flat cardboard and asking for loose change. It really does look like a tale of two cities within one. And it scares me – how did this happen to them? Drugs, drink, breakdown? All sorts of unexpected things can occur in life; I never expected to end up here like this, single and jobless, but it's happened. I don't know how I'd cope if it wasn't for the support of my family, my mother and Tara looking out for me. I feel tears rising in my eyes. How lucky I am. How much I've got.

I arrive at the taxi queue and see a woman about my own age wrapped in a dirty blanket on the kerb. There are no millionaires in Ballybeg, but never have I seen a person left in the gutter. But I'm not in Ballybeg now and I'm going to have to remember that this city doesn't look out for the needy. I open my wallet and take out a couple of spare notes, pressing them into her palm. Her eyes remain closed.

'Thanks, love.' I nearly jump out of my skin as a disembodied voice coughs and splutters from somewhere behind me.

I spin around on my heel. 'Hello?'

Movement. Shuffling. A soft-edged human-sized shape unbundles and emerges from the shadows of two chained-up wheelie bins, straightening up as he peels off his sleeping bag. 'Didn't mean to scare you.'

'No, you didn't scare me. I was just startled, that's all. I didn't see you back there.'

His accent is from down the country, just like mine. I dip my hand into my purse again, but I haven't anything more to give. 'I'm so sorry, I need this twenty for my taxi fare. I don't know what it's going to cost, otherwise you could have it.'

He waves a dismissive hand at me. He's about my age too, thirty at the most. He's bundled up in a matted woollen hat and scarf along with a few layers of stained fleece. Why on earth is he sleeping rough like this? What could have gone so wrong that he's ended up here?

I hold out my hand to introduce myself. 'Evelyn.'

'Martin,' he answers, shaking it firmly. He shoots a look down to my suitcase. 'So you've just arrived?'

I nod. 'From Ballybeg. And yourself?'

He smiles at me but doesn't attempt to answer my question. 'Do you know where you are going?'

'Yes, my sister will meet me.'

'Good, that's good. Easy to lose your way round here.'

A laughing businessman in a sharp suit steps out of a revolving glass door, a mobile tucked into the crook of his neck and a folder of documents in his hand.

Martin steps forward and begins to shout at him. 'Pieces of paper wrapped in glass and stone.' He points up to the windows of the office block and then holds up the dirty cardboard he obviously sleeps on. 'But people wrapped in paper. Don't you think there's something a bit wrong about that, Mr O'Leary? Don't you think there's something wrong about kicking human beings out of their homes and into the street and replacing them with filing cabinets and photocopiers?'

The businessman thrusts his phone in his pocket and scurries off.

'Bloody bloodsucker developer!' Martin shouts after him. But the businessman is on his phone again and doesn't look back. 'Hope you sleep well at night knowing you've thrown good people out into the street, taken away our beds, robbed us of our homes. You're ripping out the heart of this city.'

The man disappears into the crowd and Martin turns to me, shaking his head and biting down on his lip.

'Who was that?' I ask.

'Vulture developer. Council cuts on social housing, so he swoops in to buy it all up, tenants evicted, just like that. He promised we'd be rehoused, promised the earth, but once the building was his, all the promises dried up.' He nods towards the office block. 'I used to live in there, number twelve. Now I live here.' He looks down at the spot where he is standing.

I had no idea that could happen. I didn't realise that you could fall so hard and nobody would catch you. All of a sudden I feel very naive and very much out of my depth. Starting your life again is not for the weak; there's enough unpredictability in the world without shaking everything up just because you want better. Surely my situation before was more than adequate, much more than poor Martin has right now.

I'm next in the queue, and the taxi driver honks for my attention.

'I've got to go now, Martin. Let me see if I've any change at all.' I feel around but can't find anything except Nurofen and eyeliner and…

'Antiseptic spray?' I offer, blushing at the absurdity.

Martin holds up his hand. 'Nah, its grand, thanks. I'm travelling light.'

I go to take a step away, but as the cab driver loads my suitcase into the boot, I turn round again. Suddenly I want to know more about this man's story. I want to know how he got here and how he feels about it and whether I can contact anyone for him. A brother, a sister, a parent. I want to know if there's anything I can do, but I doubt he'll tell me. If he won't reveal where he's from, he's unlikely to divulge anything else personal. But there's more to find out, I just know it.

'What's it like when you sleep out at night?'

He takes a moment to consider what he wants to say, and then his strikingly bright pale-blue eyes meet mine.

'If you're dry, night-time can be magical. Amazes me that all these people scramble around glued to their little screens, looking down, always looking for inspiration, for meaning. And they're missing it. Night after night. All they've got to do is raise their faces to the sky and gaze up at the canopy of stars.'

I wait for a moment, speechless.

'Great stars on the west coast. Hope you get to see some here too.' Jutting his chin in the air, he smiles. 'Now go on, your carriage awaits.'

I step into the car, and all the way to Tara's I think about Martin and his situation. He had no choice about what life threw at him and he's not in a position to change it. The choice to split up, James and I made of our own free will. The delicious pleasure it gave me to hand my notice in at St Mary's was completely my decision. Moving up here and starting again isn't something to be afraid of; it is something to be cherished, to be thankful for, to be excited about. Not having the chance to start again – now that is scary. And I decide that from now on, every chance that comes my way is going to be met with gratitude and fearlessness, because I'm one of the lucky ones. Lucky that I get any chances at all.

CHAPTER FOUR

The taxi weaves its way through the tight traffic to Tara's flat amongst a warren of tall Georgian town houses. When we arrive, I bang on the giant knocker of the big red door and wait.

And wait.

And wait some more.

I hear movement inside, but nobody seems to be coming to the door.

I catch my reflection in the oversized mirrored chimes that tinkle in the wind beside the front door. My exhaustion is evident; my hair looks dusty, gathered into a loose knot at the back of my head, long fringe bedraggled on either side of my face like a burnt-out ballerina. Even my eyes look pale, almost ghostly and see-through, thanks to the big dark bags underneath them. Whoever answers this door is going to think it's an attack of the living dead. I try to lick down the stray hairs standing up and puff up the hairs that are flat. Give me strength.

I spent all day yesterday trying to decide what I needed to bring and squeeze it into a wheelie suitcase. The rest I'll keep stored away in my mother's garage. Luckily I don't own much. Well, not any more. The biggest portion of stuff got reassigned to the charity shop. Too many memories. James's old T-shirt that I wore to bed. The goldfish-bowl wine glasses that I envisaged us drinking from on a blanket in front of an open fire, but which in reality I drank from alone while James kept calling down the stairs that he just needed to finish this level on his game and then he'd join me. But by the time he was ready, I was spent. Just never seemed to come together.

I sit down on the suitcase and take out my phone to check again that I've got the right address. Then I double-check my sister's text message.

Cannot wait! Will be at the door with bells on. You just get yourself up here and we'll take care of everything else. Dog days are over, babe, let the fun begin. Love you xx

So she knows I'm coming. She's expecting me. I knock once more. Still no answer.

I sit down again and consider my options. This is Day One of Project Zero, starting my life all over again. I can't go home; I've already lined up an interview with a recruitment agency that I absolutely need to attend if I'm ever going to carve a living for myself outside of Ballybeg. I can't make the return journey within hours of leaving – that's just embarrassing. And I don't really have anywhere else to go... which is a very depressing thought.

I text Tara: *Where are you?* No reply. I give her a ring, but her phone is turned off, which normally means she's up in the air. Head in the clouds. Literally. Tara isn't a planner; everything she does is slapdash and scribbled down somewhere on a scrap of paper. It's usually organised chaos, but clearly not today.

I look to the sky. A shamrock-emblazoned plane cuts across the city skyline in the distance. She could be on that one. I bloody well hope not, though, as it's just taken off and looks like its heading across the Irish Sea.

Maybe I should do that too.

I've got my passport, I've got some cash. Perhaps the idea of coming to stay with Tara was just daft. After all, I could do anything. I could go anywhere. I have no husband or job to consider. I'm all by myself with no one to answer to. Maybe I should have set my sights a bit further afield; gone to London, invested all my savings in some madcap business I saw on

Dragons' Den and become a workaholic entrepreneur millionaire. Or tried my luck on a sheep farm in New Zealand, living alone out in the rolling hills, roaming the land each day with my staff and my trusty dog. Or crushed grapes with my bare feet in the vineyards of France by day and got suitably plastered with the other labourers at night. Or maybe I should just go to a petrol station toilet, shave all my hair off and join the army like Katy Perry did in her post-break-up video.

I shake this nonsense out of my head. I know myself too well to even entertain these fantasies. I am a complete scaredy-cat. I want to stay in Ireland because it's my home and I belong here, and ideally I want to stay being a teacher because it's the one thing I know I can do. When things were going so wrong with James and I had to question myself about absolutely everything, from whether I was attractive enough to whether I was trying hard enough to make it work, the one thing that made me feel competent and worthy again was standing up in front of a class and having some sort of control. Knowing I could do it. Connecting and engaging; in my classes each day, I felt happy. I felt alive. I need to go to this interview tomorrow and get back into my happy place, because at least I know I can't fail at that.

And as for moving to Dublin, this is as far as I've ever really got from my west-coast village and the first time I've done anything remotely grown-up on my own.

Has everything I thought I had really gone? Is everything I thought I knew really wrong?

I need to make this work. I'm not putting my life on hold any more. That's all I've done for the past few months. Today is the day I stop waiting.

I've got to embrace this change. The worst is over, the decision is made, the paperwork is underway and I'm stepping into my new life, whatever it may hold, because you know what? I'm ready. I'm ready and I'm excited, and it's weird, because I always thought free-falling like this would feel terrifying, but actually it feels a bit like flying. And I'm starting to like that feeling very much. This is my plan and I need it to work. So I'm not going anywhere until somebody answers this door and lets me know what on earth is going on.

I take a deep breath and straighten my back. I want some answers. God knows, I've asked enough questions.

CHAPTER FIVE

Where on earth is Tara? I step up to the door and bang the knocker really hard again. Then I crouch down to the letter box and snap it open. 'Hello? Anybody in?'

'For feck's sake, what is it now? I swear I'm going to murder someone,' shouts a gravelly voice inside, harsh and angry.

I hear stomping down the stairs. Then the door swings open and a hunched old woman with bushy white eyebrows is standing there, a gang of straight-tailed cats circling her feet. She curls her lip at me in confusion.

'You're not a Jehovah's Witness?'

I shake my head. 'I'm Evelyn… Tara's sister. I'm supposed to move in today – just for a while, till I get myself set up. But she's not here and I've got all my stuff…'

A flicker of recognition. 'Oh, of course! The divorced one… Aren't men BASTARDS?' Her hands fly to her mouth. 'Come in this minute. Let me take your bags, you've been through enough.'

I follow her up the stairs, careful not to step on a cat or trip over stacks of unopened post.

'I'm Moira, the landlady. I live up here with my granddaughter.' She points to a closed door behind her, then places a long-nailed finger to her lips. 'Still in bed, the lazy sod, that's teenagers for you. No getting through to that one, just trouble and drama, sulking and slamming doors.' She flutters her hand above her head.

I look round Moira's living room. There is no sign of a teenager living here at all. The sofa is covered in tiger-print cushions, and a daytime chat show flashes on the screen of the TV in the corner. Moira clears a coffee table covered with crosswords and word-search puzzles.

'None of your girls are downstairs at the moment – air hostesses come and go at all manner of times. I never know where they are. They're good girls, though, especially your sister. I'm usually very strict on one person per room, but seeing as it's Tara, I made an exception. Sit down and we'll have a drink. One of them should be home soon enough to let you in.'

She waves me to the sofa, then lights up a fag, opens a box of red wine and sloshes two glasses full.

'So, what are your plans now that you are here?'

'Get settled, get myself set up. Hopefully once I've got a job and start earning, I'll be able to get my own place, start my life here.'

'I admire you. It's not easy. My own husband upped and left me, you know, when I was your age…' Three cats jump into her lap, and she kisses each of them on the mouth. 'And that was that. I was a sullied woman. Second-hand goods. Why on earth would a man court me, another man's cast-off, when he could choose someone without baggage?'

She offers me a cat. I decline. What's she telling me? That I'm finished? That it's not a matter of moving to the city or changing my life; the rule is that you get one shot to be happy in love, and if you mess it up, then it's game over? No. No way. That can't be true.

'Really? There are people who think like that?' I ask her.

She slaps my thigh. 'I'm joking! Gorgeous girl like yourself, you are going to have the best time of all!' She blinks slowly. 'That's what I've done. *Never a wife, always a mistress be.* That's my motto. I have gentlemen callers aplenty, dinners, theatre, gifts, you name it. All the romance happens outside of marriage, believe me. Once two people know that they can be free to be themselves – that's when the magic starts. And if you're looking for magic, Dublin is the place for you.' She winks at me.

'Anytime you want to call up here for a little wine and a chat, you're welcome, okay? We could have a right chinwag, me and you. We could go out.' She taps her finger against her nose. 'I'll show you all the best places to find eligible men.'

'Definitely,' I lie. Out on the prowl with Moira? I think that really would be rock bottom.

'So you're a teacher, I hear? That's a nice number. Great holidays; you seem to be off more than you're at work. I hate school holidays and weekends and evenings. Impossible to keep kids busy. Teenagers are always complaining, always bored, always wanting money or getting into trouble...' She glances up at me, her eyes widening. 'Have you a job lined up?'

'Not exactly. I've got an appointment with a recruitment agency tomorrow, so.'

She claps her hands together. 'Oh, they'll take forever by the time they sort their paperwork. I have an idea. Why don't you tutor my granddaughter?'

I open my mouth to answer, but Moira leans forward and has both hands on my knee now, staring at me intently.

'She needs extra help, and Lord knows I can't give it to her. You're a teacher with time on your hands, living just downstairs. Couldn't be more perfect! I'll pay you. Actually, I'll take it off Tara's rent; how's that for a deal?'

I take a moment to gather my thoughts. This could be perfect; it would tide me over until I got a job, and putting 'private tutor' on my CV wouldn't do any harm. This might be just what I'm after.

'How old is your granddaughter?' I ask.

'Seventeen. About to do her final exams.'

'What kind of tutoring does she need? I'm a music teacher, so I'm not sure if I'll be qualified to help her.'

Moira rolls her eyes. 'Oh, whatever you can do will be a help, believe me. I need someone to keep her on track, off the streets.'

Right, this is sounding like a completely different kind of job...

'Could I meet her first? Introduce myself, have a little chat.'

Moira purses her lips and slants her gaze towards me. 'Evelyn, I think this is an offer you should consider carefully.' The big tomcat claws at a smaller cat under the table, causing it to scramble behind my foot, whimpering. 'As I said, I don't usually like more than one person per room… I'd hate to see you go so soon.'

Right, it's like that then. Unless I take the tutoring job, she's going to chuck me out. So it looks like I'm not left with much choice. I need to stay here with Tara, not just for somewhere to lay my head, but because I don't know a single soul in this city. I've got to be near her for moral support.

I hold out my hand to Moira. 'Looks like we have a deal,' I tell her.

She shakes my hand and nods her approval. 'Wonderful. She'll be delighted. I'll call down during the week and let you know the times that will suit. I think this could make the world of difference to her. Keep her busy and out of harm's way.' She empties the last of the wine box into her own glass. 'Another drink?' she offers, waving the empty box. I politely decline, shaking my head and wondering what on earth I've got myself into.

Suddenly I hear footsteps on the stairs, and Tara rushes in through the door behind me, waving her gratitude to Moira. 'I'm so sorry. Flight delayed, and then stuck in traffic! How are you?'

My sister's lovely excited face is a breath of fresh air. Even though she is technically late, this is perfect timing. I understand even more now how much I need her, how much there is to learn and how quickly I will need to find my feet. She wraps her arms around me, and her scent, the touch of her hair, her skin is so comforting, I feel like a small part of me is home.

I kiss her over and over on her forehead, stroking her cheeks. 'It is so good to see you,' I tell her, tears starting to well in my eyes.

She thanks Moira for looking after me, and leads me down to her ground-floor flat.

*

When Tara said I should come to stay with her until I got set up, I had no idea that she lived like an actual adult in a very modern, stylish and homely two-bedroom flat. The place is spotless. There's a huge Frida Kahlo framed print above a redundant fireplace, and a glass coffee table with a vase of fresh red and yellow flowers. It looks more like it belongs to a professional couple than a flat share. I love it.

'That's Inez's room,' she says as she points at the first bedroom. 'She works all hours, mainly long haul too, so you'll hardly see her. But we'll arrange a night out together once our shifts have settled down. Bring you out on the town!' She swivels on the spot and spins towards a second door. She pushes it open and waves her hand with a flourish at the tiny box room. 'And...' I take in the tight single bed and a lopsided wardrobe bursting at the seams, 'this is us. Welcome to your new abode!'

She flops on the mattress. 'Right, you, make yourself at home. I know it's a bit of a squeeze, but we'll be grand! Dooley girls together again!'

'Thank you, Tara. It's wonderful.'

She raises an eyebrow. 'C'mon, we both know it's not ideal, but it's a start, right?' She pats the blanket beside her. 'You're here. You've made it. I'm so proud of you, Evelyn. Really.'

She loops a stray tendril of hair away from my cheek and around my ear. God, it's good to be close to her, to have my sister on my side again.

'So how does it feel? Are you excited?' she asks me.

'Yes, absolutely!' I try to echo her enthusiasm, but surprise myself at the tiny crack in my voice.

'Tell me.' I sit by her and she rubs my back. 'You look a bit... sad.'

I bite down and swallow hard. I was so trying not to look sad. I am trying not to *be* sad. I am trying to override anything that is operating on a frequency beneath gung-ho positivity. I thought I was doing quite a good job on that front. Note to self: don't bother trying to deceive Tara. She'll get me every time. But the last thing I want is for her to worry about me; she's got her own life and she's really happy and successful, and I don't want to be a burden to her, moving in here all lost and wary like a big Eeyore. A fat tear spills down my cheek.

'We've got to get you out and about again. Get your mojo back.'

'I don't have a problem with going out. I can't wait to go out! I'm just emotional. I never thought I'd be here like this. I thought I had it all mapped out, you know – husband, house, job. And now they're all gone. But here I am with you, so thank you, Tara. Thank you for edging me towards this. Thank you for knowing this is what I needed.'

Tara's eyes widen and she clicks her tongue just like she used to do as a little girl every time she had a brainwave or an inspired idea. 'I want to show you something.' She hops up to turn off the light switch and draws the curtains as tight as she can. 'Now, look up.'

I lift my gaze, and see a freckling of plastic glow-in-the-dark stars glued to the ceiling.

'I cannot believe you still have these,' I tell her as I get up from the bed and reach my hand towards them.

After our father died, I became obsessed with the universe. A teacher at school had explained that energy could not be destroyed, only transferred, so I convinced myself that Dad had simply transferred from matter into light. One night in our bunks, shortly after Tara's tenth birthday, she declared that she did not believe in ghosts. If Dad had any way to communicate with us, she said, then he would. He'd prank us and send us little messages of love. So because he didn't do it, that meant there was no such things as ghosts.

I hadn't realised that all the same thoughts that were going around my head were also going around hers. Where had he gone? Where was he now? Could he see us? How would we know? Why did he have to go in the first place?

'I think that makes sense. I don't believe in ghosts either,' I told her. 'But...'

She bolted upwards, eager to hear, waiting for some hopeful explanation that would make our absent dad feel closer.

'I believe that he's a star, and that he's still around, even though we can't see him. The universe is so deep, it can hold an unlimited number of stars. It has mysteries we can't even begin to fathom.'

After school the next day, I glued these tiny plastic stars to the ceiling above Tara's bunk, so that if she ever felt lonely, all she had to do was look up and remember what we'd said. That the stars only appeared to fade away, but really they were there all the time, indestructible points of energy shining above us always.

'They were the first thing I put up when I moved here. They made the place more friendly somehow.' She squeezes my knee. 'I wish you had told me you were so unhappy. Cry it out now; I think you've been holding on to it for too long by yourself.'

There's no point trying to kid Tara. If there is anyone I can open up to, it's her; after all, we're sisters – she can't exactly divorce me.

'I didn't even want myself to know, I suppose. I was so sure I would be better off without James, but it's still new, and sometimes it's weird being on my own. It's a roller coaster: excited one minute, terrified the next. Confused, conflicted, crazy. How is it that I miss him?'

'You just miss the *idea* of him, of what you thought you had. You did the right thing.'

'Really?' I raise my eyebrows. Apart from the marriage counsellor, Tara is the first person to say this to me. Everyone else has made me feel like I've made a huge mistake.

She takes both my hands in hers. 'Remember when we were kids, you used to hold a festival, creating all those little shows, and then we'd sell tickets and you'd decorate the tree house with lights and bunting and every kid in the village would come, and there'd be music and dancing and tables stacked high with crisps and sandwiches. Dad would always sing.'

I nod my head and smile. Dad loved a good old sing-song. The old folk songs especially – traditional Irish songs of love and history and working fields and crossing seas and, of course, loss. I rub my forehead, trying to wipe the memory away. Why are we even talking about this? I thought she was trying to cheer me up.

'What's the festival got to do with James?'

'Exactly. Nothing. That was just you, Evelyn. Your dreams, your decisions, your destiny. Then James came into your life and kind of took you over…' She rubs her hands together, careful about what she says next. 'I guess what I'm saying is that you are more than Mum's daughter or James's wife or the local teacher. You are Evelyn Dooley – bright and beautiful and creative and organised and quirky and so, so kind. I want you to find your voice again, and you will, I promise you. And the second you find it, follow it with all your heart.'

As much as it hurts, I know that what Tara is telling me is right. And I've got to own up to this despite how easy it would be to blame James. I let myself be taken over; I adored him so much and everyone was so happy about us being together that I slipped into the role of happy homemaker and shelved everything else. I stopped going out with my own friends, I stopped playing my instruments, I stopped travelling to the places I wanted to go and doing the things I used to love to do, and then of course I resented James or my job or the work on the cottage for that happening. But a lot of it was down to me. And I'm so sorry for that. I vow I will never let it happen again.

I've cried a lot over the past couple of years. Always by myself, behind closed doors, into my pillow. And I thought I'd made a good job of hiding it, but now the tears gush forth and I just let them, not even trying to wipe them away.

Tara takes my hands in hers. 'This is the beginning of a brand-new story – this time one with a happy ending.'

And as I let my little sister hold me, I feel happy and complete and excited for the first time in as long as I can remember. I know better than to break this silence, rare and unguarded as it is. I wrap my arms around her neck and listen to the gentle thrum of her heart – the kind of sound that can only be heard very, very close-up.

Soon it's time to turn off the lights, and we lie top to tail, just as we did when we were little girls and our heads were full of dreams. With Tara already snoring beside me, I gather the blankets in a ball under my chin and think about tomorrow, such a big day ahead. A day of chasing dreams and seizing chances and starting my brand-new story. And I smile, my heart settling in my chest as I gaze up at the glow-in-the dark stars above that are shining just for me.

CHAPTER SIX

It's only seven in the morning and already I've gone way too far. Long skinny lines, no shape, no curve. I survey the chaotic mess of my sister's bedside locker: pens, Post-its, make-up-remover wipes, an impressive array of painkillers. And of course, Tara's light-up tweezers. Definitely a duty-free impulse buy, which I had to impulsively try out, promising myself I'd exercise restraint and just go for a little tidy-up around the edges. What harm could come from a little brow-scaping before an important interview?

Big mistake. Huge, giant, colossal mistake.

I'm dressed in my best suit, and I've got all my qualifications in my briefcase. I've got a travel card, directions and spare shoes. I was pretty much ready to take on the world until I spotted the tweezers – my kryptonite. I just couldn't resist a quick pluck.

And once I started, I couldn't stop.

Now I'm left with these horrifically sparse, patchy lines where my brows used to be. People think it matters what you wear, how you speak, and apparent status symbols like your watch or your handbag. Nope. In my opinion, it's hardest to charm your way out of lousy eyebrows. Eyebrows make a statement. If the eyes are the window to the soul, the eyebrows are the all-important signposts that arch over them.

I shiver as I check my own poor emaciated brows. They will take at least a week to grow out. And I've got an interview! You only get one chance to make a first impression, and I really don't want the recruitment consultant to think I'm auditioning to be a pantomime dame. Next week, I'll be back to sporting my Cara Delevingne luxury brows; judge me then.

I have little choice but to pull and feather my fringe forward to camouflage the entire top half of my face, before tottering down the cobbled path from our front door into the busy city street. As I dash past rows of cosy red-brick terraces, I breathe in the scent of fried bacon and buttered toast, which reminds me of my mother. She'll be thinking of me this morning, lighting candles and muttering prayers to St Gerard under her breath. St Gerard, the patron saint of new beginnings; let's hope he's been listening.

I flag my bus and the driver wishes me good morning with a big smile. I take the front seat and he agrees happily to let me know where to get off. I thank him and look out of the window as my new neighbourhood wakes up along with my own sense of excitement, the new-found sense of pride I feel rising up inside me. I'm here. I'm doing this. And I start to believe that today may be salvageable after all – even if my poor old eyebrows are not.

Jumping off at my stop downtown, I am met at the office door by Gavin, the recruitment agent. Even though he smells of egg fart and industrial bleach, I smile at him while trying to breathe through my mouth. He slides my CV from my hand and wheezes all over it. Gavin looks somewhat the worse for wear, like he may be a bit hung-over, or indeed, still drunk.

'Good morning, Miss Dooley – all shiny and new up from the country!' He glances down at my details. 'Ballybeg, now that is the back end of beyond. Well you are in luck, because,' he leans in conspiratorially and cups his hand to his mouth, 'we do like country girls like yourself around here. Hard workers, not afraid to put their backs into it, if you follow me.'

I don't follow him. Unless he means that he pays country girls less because they don't know any better.

'How's life treating you so far in the big city, eh? We have people like you arrive all the time. Up to the big smoke, they think, ah sure, I'll be grand. Dublin's only a few hours up the motorway – how different can it be?'

His smile slips from his face and he lowers his tone. 'But then the reality sinks in. The expense, the competition, the crime, the anonymity, the loneliness. You may have been a big fish in a small pond before, but now you are not even a fish, Evelyn – you are plankton... in a filthy, filthy pond. Have you seen the River Liffey? Full of syringes and shopping trolleys. No joke, worst I've ever seen.'

He takes me by the elbow and leads me to a seat. I can feel the heat of his sweaty palm through my clothes. Then he stretches back in his own chair.

'So, some advice if you want to survive in this place, sweetheart. Don't be out late at night on your own, keep your belongings close to your person at all times, and basically, don't trust anyone. Especially drunks and recruitment agents.' He nearly chokes on his own joke, then waves over to a guy in a suit by the water cooler. 'Isn't that right, Deano? Young teacher here up from the country; she'll be eaten alive if she hasn't her wits about her.'

Deano, a sickly pallor to his skin, salutes with a shaky hand.

Gavin leans over the table to me. 'You know, I could show you around if you wanted... strictly professional, of course. We could go for a little spin in the company car and I could show you the areas you want to work in, full of the beautiful people – I could see you slotting in there nicely. Give you a leg-up, if you know what I mean.'

He pauses, but I don't laugh. What kind of a place is this? It's sweaty, it's sleazy, it stinks of bad breath and booze. I realise now that that's probably the reason why I got an appointment here so quickly: not because there is a desperate teacher shortage, but because this whole set-up is a complete joke. I decide to give it five more minutes, and if he can't offer me anything worthwhile, I'll just leave. Cut my losses and try another agency. Only thing is, there aren't too many other agencies to choose from on this side of the city.

Gavin leans back in his seat, waving a hand towards the window. 'I'll even show you the rough side of town. What would you think of that, Evelyn? All the dangerous areas that a good wholesome girl like you has never been in before. Probably never imagined in your wildest nightmares… Strictly professional, of course. What do you say?' He runs a tongue over his bottom lip. And he stays that way, like a dazed dog.

'Is that something you do with everyone who comes in here? Give them a one-to-one tour?' I ask.

He shakes his head, smiling at me. 'No! Not at all! Just for very special clients – ones I think could use a little extra… orientation. I'm passionate about my job, you see. I imagine that you are very passionate too, am I right, Ms Dooley?'

What a creep. I need to get out of here. I need to cut to the chase and stop wasting precious time.

'Have you got any actual vacancies at the moment? I want to start work in a school as soon as possible – I really don't mind if it's considered a good area or not.'

He raises his eyes at me like I've just said something cute but ridiculously naive.

'Kids are kids, people are people, I'll be happy anywhere. I just want to get started asap.'

Gavin runs a greasy finger across the top of my CV. 'Bad time of year for teachers – halfway through the term. In about six weeks' time, there'll be a glut of work, people moving jobs, school trips, maybe even a maternity leave… that's when you'll get something, but right now, there's nothing. Bone dry. If you'll excuse me.'

He looks over to the water cooler and unbuttons his collar. 'Feeling a bit delicate today; we celebrated Deano's birthday last night.'

I nod my understanding and watch him cross the office.

Six weeks is a long time with no income. I have savings, but that won't last long if I don't have a job. I don't know how long it will take to sell the cottage and release all the investment I've poured into that. Sometimes these things take forever, so I can't risk spending money I don't actually have.

I definitely need something. Maybe Gavin has some jobs in more difficult areas that he thinks I won't be able to cope with because I'm new to the city. Maybe he thinks I'm too inexperienced. I bite down on my lip. I'm here to begin again, and I want to begin now. I pick up my bag and follow Gavin over to the water cooler, where he's leaning against the wall, eyes closed. He's not a good colour.

'Anything at all, I don't mind where it is or what it is. Just something to tide me over until a more suitable post comes up. I can handle myself, I promise you that.'

He shakes his head and fans himself with my CV. 'As I said, bad timing for teachers.'

And with that, he hiccups, both his cheeks blow out and his hands fly up to clasp his mouth. He runs to the bathroom, and I can hear from the splash and groan that he makes it just in time.

I stand alone in the middle of the agency. The only person who is worse than Gavin at recruitment is the person who recruited him in the first place.

I sling my coat over my shoulder and walk out into the swarming street outside. I'm jostled by people on every side, coming at me in all directions. People going to work. People eating breakfast, drinking coffee, talking on their phones, laughing with their colleagues, discussing their work, their homes, their relationships, building them, growing them. I'm struck with admiration, with respect for these people living their lives, making their plans, taking one courageous step after another. All these people on their way.

Except me. I stand in the midst of them and wonder what I should do next. What I *can* do next.

My phone beeps. It's a text from Mum.

Lit candle for you this morning. Hope day goes well. Parish are going to Rome on a visit. I've put my name down. Want to say hello to the Pope in person. How's job hunt going? Mum xx

Even my mother is going places. Job hunt indeed. By the looks of it, I am going to have to hunt one down myself. Six weeks is a long time to do absolutely nothing but wait for Gavin to sort me out – if he's even capable of doing that. Six weeks is a long time to be under your flatmates' feet without role or purpose. Six weeks is a long time to be skint in a new place and not go out to pubs or clubs or theatres or even pay for a bus ticket home. I need to find something. Anything. Not in six weeks' time, but now.

CHAPTER SEVEN

I spend the rest of the morning getting on and off buses, going in and out of every other teacher recruitment agency there is. On the one hand, it is a fantastic way to get around Dublin, to get to know my bearings and bus routes and the names of new streets and landmarks. On the other hand, it is complete shite because it appears Gavin was right – every single recruitment agent I meet says the same thing: wrong time of the year for teacher vacancies.

I leave my CV with the last agency on my list and just start walking, following the river as it flows through the middle of the city. I walk along ancient cobbled alleys, past shop windows and the Molly Malone statue, back over the Ha'Penny bridge through Temple Bar and on towards Trinity, past castles, cathedrals and courthouses. I keep walking up Grafton Street with its flower sellers and street musicians, mime artists and buskers, until I reach the top and find a bench tucked away in a shady corner of St Stephen's Green. A couple on a picnic blanket by the pond are laughing as they feed the ducks and share a punnet of strawberries.

James and I were like that once, two people in love who laughed, made plans, made promises to each other. But then it fell apart. Nobody's fault. Nobody to blame. Unforeseen limits to our capacities. On the inside, we could not know what was happening; it was so much bigger than us. Two immature kids who took on too much without enough of a solid foundation to build upon. We signed ourselves over to each other without giving a thought to finding out who we actually were. What

I knew of love was what had been shown to me, and what I'd learned from all those saccharine big-screen fairy tales; neither model was very realistic. Even if we'd known what to expect, I don't think it would've changed much. I hope he's okay. I hope he's still having fun. I hope the Ibiza scene is everything he hoped it would be.

I pull out my hair from its tight bun and try to shake thoughts of the past, of James, of false steps and disappointments out of my mind. Enough, it's gone, let it lie. What good is going over old ground? It dawns on me that my thoughts stray to the dark side when I'm tired, hungry or premenstrual. Right now I'm all three. It's probably best I head home, call into Moira's and try to learn a bit more about her granddaughter, do a bit of swotting-up before we have our first official tuition session.

I get off the bus and head towards Tara's street, stopping on the corner when I spot an old-fashioned pub. I'm sure this is where Tara and her friends used to drink when she started her training; I remember her crazy tales of late nights and lock-ins at Rosie Munroe's. At the time, it made me slightly envious. I wanted to be with Tara as she improvised her own version of *Riverdance* or locked eyes with a smouldering stranger across the bar. Sometimes it left me with a sinking feeling that I might have settled down a little too quickly and missed out on the chance to meet new people and broaden my horizons. Missed out on the chance to find myself in a brand-new setting, without the safety net of the familiar.

Sunlight splashes on the ornate white stucco, and pale green leaves creep up the walls and around the windows. It's lunchtime, my feet hurt and I'm parched from all the walking and talking I've done this morning. So in I go to the pub with its peeling red and black sign. *Tea, coffee, fresh hand-cut sandwiches* is scrawled in chalk on the blackboard outside. Yes, I could definitely do with that. I'm starving.

This pub is one of Dublin's few remaining traditional drinking dens – no plasma screens showing news and sport, no blaring music, just a single one-armed bandit flashing gently. It's nice in here, quiet and cosy. There are a few old flat-capped men sitting in one corner, bent over their pints contemplating life and tapping their calloused fingers along with the faint traditional music playing in the background. I settle at the end of the bar, gazing out through the stained-glass window, entranced by the way the sunlight lifts the greens and the reds, like in a church. I order a large coffee and a toasted cheese sandwich from a barman with a limp and a sling.

'Coffee and toasted sandwich?' He squints at me with despair.

'Yes please, if that's all right.'

He holds up his bandaged fingers. 'It's a bit tricky with this, you see. And my part-timer has just called in sick. I had to fire my full-timer, and my emergency backup has had an emergency. So, would half a Guinness and a packet of crisps tide you over instead?'

I nod. 'That sounds lovely. Bit early for a drink, but I guess it's not like I've anywhere to be.'

He pours my Guinness, the flood of creamy white into black like a slow tide reminding me of my home by the ocean.

'Nowhere to be? You look like you're a lawyer or a politician or something.' I shake my head and he looks over my shoulder and lowers his voice to a whisper. 'Or maybe you're up in court?'

'Not at all!' I laugh. 'Recruitment meeting. But I need a job for six weeks until something comes through. Who hires for six weeks, right?'

'Ah, you'd be surprised. What line of work are you in?'

'I'm a teacher, a music teacher.'

He holds out his right hand. 'Colm Munroe, pleased to meet you.'

I introduce myself and take the first delicious cold, velvety sip of my Guinness, licking the white moustache from my top lip. 'After the morning I've had, this feels like a real treat. Much better than a coffee, so thank you.'

Colm turns to the only other customer at the counter, a silver-haired man with a large glass of whiskey in front of him. 'Do you know anyone who needs a music teacher, Christy? Evelyn here is looking for work.'

Christy shakes his head. 'Work is hard to come by these days, unless you're into computers. Loads of jobs in that line. Music not so much.'

'I'll just have to hope something comes up.'

'It will, just give it time. If it's for you, it won't pass you by,' Colm says with a warm smile.

I relax into my seat. 'That's a favourite line of my mother's.'

'Well your mother must be a very wise woman. I believe in it myself; plenty of truth in the old sayings. I know it's not very modern to believe in fate or destiny, but I do.'

Christy blows out his cheeks and raises his eyes to the heavens. 'Colm, I swear you are getting dafter by the day. Destiny now, is it? I've never heard anything so ridiculous.'

'Master plan written in the sky for us all, Christy,' Colm tells him as he wipes the counter with his good hand.

'Absolute nonsense. Everything that happens in our lives happens as a result of our own doing and a bit of luck. Or bad luck, as the case may be.'

Colm shakes his head. 'You're wrong, Christy. That particular philosophy holds that we have control of our lives, or indeed our actions. And that's another thing. Yes, you may feel like you woke up this morning and chose to spend the day drinking on that stool, but in fact it's a false choice. Sure, you are wired to it.'

Christy licks his lips and pushes out his empty glass. 'You might have a point there. Top her up.' He laughs.

Colm pours out the last measure in the bottle. 'I'll need to go and restock the spirits. Will you keep an eye on the place?'

We both nod and he disappears down a hatch into the cellar.

Once Colm is out of earshot, whiskered Christy leans towards me and lowers his voice to a gravelly hush. 'This place is too much for him now. He's not well, not that he'll admit it. See his hand? He fainted out the back lifting kegs and broke his fingers. I told him he needs to slow down, get some help in, but he won't listen. Stubborn mule.'

I look around. There must be seating for over a hundred in here, but other than the few old guys in the corner, there are no other customers. 'I suppose he thinks he can manage,' I offer.

Christy nods. 'Catch twenty-two. Slow business means skeleton staff, which means even fewer customers and less money to invest in the decor, in music nights and decent publicity, and then it's just a downward spiral from there. This place could be a gold mine if only someone put some heart into it. Oldest pub in Dublin this.'

'Really?' I glance upwards to the shelving behind the bar, where assorted antiques and photographs remind me of my own father's local back in Ballybeg. Vintage Guinness posters, battered hurley sticks and signed Gaelic football jerseys, old-style blue and white Delft serving dishes alongside horseshoes and sepia photos of smiling old men in flat caps playing tin whistles and accordions.

Christy points to a framed photo in the corner. 'Go in behind the bar there, Evelyn, and pass down that photograph.'

I raise my eyebrows. Really? It's a sacred space, like backstage at the theatre or the sacristy of a church. 'I can't do that. Surely behind the bar is authorised personnel only.'

Christy rolls his eyes and waves his hand. 'Not at all, Colm won't mind. I want you to see that picture. Brilliant it is.'

'Okay,' I concede. I want to see this picture too, and I've never been behind a bar before. Spent plenty of time drinking, obviously, but never serving. I slip behind the old wooden counter and reach up on my tiptoes to fetch the dusty photo frame, handing it to Christy.

'See here. Must be fifty years old now.' He wipes the glass with his sleeve. 'There she is. Colm's aunt, Rosie Munroe herself. The infamous landlady. What do you notice about this picture?'

I study the scene, recognising the bar, two women beaming proudly either side of this very counter. I run my hand across the wood, imagining Rosie Munroe standing in this exact spot half a century ago.

'I'll tell you the story of this picture. In the late sixties, women weren't allowed to be served in a pub unless a man ordered their drink. And they were only allowed a spirit or a soft drink at that. If they ordered a pint, they were refused. So what did Rosie do? In 1969, she organised a pub crawl of thirty women and my own father. Growing up side by side, our families have been close for generations. He went with them from pub to pub, ordering thirty brandies. They were served. And they drank them. And then Rosie'd order a pint of Guinness, and she was refused. In every pub they went to, the same thing happened.'

I'm fascinated. I've never thought about the restrictions on women in my own mother's lifetime, the thought that she'd have to have a man order something as simple as a drink. Here I am, sitting on my own with a Guinness in the middle of the day and nobody blinks an eyelid. What a tremendous change in one generation.

'I've never heard of Rosie Munroe before. What happened next?'

Christy takes a long slug of his whiskey to lubricate his vocal cords. 'Well, if Rosie couldn't find a way, she'd make a way. She took over the bar here, put her own name above the door – the only pub with a woman's name on the licence this side of the river – and did as she liked.'

'So she just ignored the law and served women anyway?' I ask.

Christy shook his head. 'Not at all, they'd have shut her down. The law said you couldn't sell pints to women, but it didn't say you couldn't give them pints for free.' He taps his finger on the photograph. 'So this is what she's doing right here. The first pint served and drunk at the bar by a woman in Ireland.' He bangs the counter. 'Right where we're sitting today.'

Colm shouts up from the cellar. 'Christy, will you ask that busker outside to give me a hand. I need help shifting something.'

Christy lifts up from his seat and calls back, 'I can't hear him out there today, Colm. No sign yet, I'm afraid.'

'I can help,' I offer.

Christy shrugs and says, 'Why not? No point in talking about women's liberation and then saying this is no job for a lady, right?'

I smile. 'Dead right.' And I take the dark stairwell down into the cellar.

I volunteer to do a few jobs for Colm to help him out, mostly running errands that involve two hands – loading and emptying the dishwasher, securing the optics and screwing in a new bulb just above the till. I change the barely audible music for him once the CD finishes and put a new battery in the little speaker. All simple jobs but ones I enjoy none the less. Since turning my world upside down, I've felt like I've been on the receiving end of other people's help and kindness, so being on the other side of that, being in a position to help someone else, feels great, like I'm finally getting somewhere.

As I wash my hands under the tap and get ready to make my way home, Colm turns to me. 'You've been a great help to me today, Evelyn. I really appreciate it. I hope you'll call in to us regularly. You are very welcome here any time.'

The sentiment moves me deeply. To be invited back, to be considered a friend by these two seasoned Dubliners when I've only just arrived in the city, is so comforting. Despite all the harshness I've seen so far, here are these two discussing destiny, celebrating equality and welcoming lone strays like myself into their little kingdom.

Christy hands me the photo of Rosie Munroe. 'You wouldn't mind putting that back up before you go? I like to keep it in a safe place; it's the only copy we have.'

I take one last look at it. Rosie Munroe, what a brave and fierce woman you were. Imagine knowing your own worth so well that you'd risk everything to make sure you took your rightful place in the world. Standing here right now, in this bar, with her image in my hand, I can't quite explain it but I feel more sure, more passionate, more fired up about myself and my life and my purpose than I ever have before.

I don't want to go home. I don't want to go job-hunting tomorrow. I don't want to hand in my CV and try to sell myself and beg for scraps of work that may or may not come in. I'd rather be here. I feel I belong here.

'Colm? I have a proposition for you.' He looks up from stacking chairs one-handed by the unlit fireplace. He wipes the sweat from his brow with his hanky and tries to catch his breath, even though the heavy lifting is minimal.

'What would you say about me coming to work here? A few hours every day. I could do any jobs you need – serve customers, give you a break if you need it, anything really.'

Colm furrows his brow. 'That can't be right; sure you're a qualified teacher. We couldn't have you pulling pints and wiping counters. I appreciate the offer, Evelyn, but you've got a great profession – just give it time, something will come up. You can't throw away all that training to work in a place like this.'

I shake my head. Colm turning me down wasn't something I was expecting. He is in such clear need of help, I thought he'd bite my hand off. But now that the idea has been planted in my head, I see it is exactly the kind of opportunity I hoped a big, bold leap into the unknown would deliver. I'd love to come here every day, spend time with these two, hear their stories, join in with their chat. This is the perfect place for me to have a bit of down time, a neutral place to think about my future and regroup without career stress or taking on too much responsibility. It's at the top of the street from the flat, so I can walk here and back every day, and even a minimum wage will be enough to cover me alongside Moira's tuition job.

I can help make the place a bit better, maybe even attract some more customers in. Who knows where this might lead?

But what I do know is that it feels right. I just need to convince Colm.

'Give me a trial, Colm. I'll do a couple of shifts, and if at any stage you think it's not working, we'll call it a day. How does that sound?'

Colm is dabbing the handkerchief behind his ears, still sweating from overexertion on his light task.

Christy slams his hand down on the counter, then looks upwards, blessing himself. 'Sweet Mary, mother of God, I'm nearly beginning to believe in destiny myself! Help is at hand, Colm, staring you in the face! Take it, man; you'll not get another offer like this any time soon.' He holds out his hand to me, but I can see that Colm is still unsure.

'I don't know,' he says. 'I appreciate the offer, but can you even pull a pint?'

'I can if you show me,' I tell him. 'I'm a fast learner.'

'Destiny, Colm. There's a master plan in the sky for us all – it was a wise man that told me that once.' Christy winks at me.

'A trial period, you say?' Colm says.

I nod. 'Yes, and if it doesn't work, at least we tried, no hard feelings.'

'Right so, seeing as you're keen, it's worth a shot. Come in tomorrow at midday and we'll start training you up.'

Christy lets out a loud cheer and we high-five. 'I have a good feeling about this,' he says. 'Welcome to Rosie's, Evelyn.' And he slaps me on the back.

I have a job. Nothing like what I expected when I left the house this morning, but it's still a job. A new, exciting, completely different job for me. And I don't just feel relief that the job hunt is over for a while; I feel privileged treading the same boards as the late great Rosie Munroe. Proud to serve in her pub, to take her place behind the counter, to be surrounded by her legacy.

It makes me feel a little bit invincible. And a little bit fierce and fearless and all-out fired up for all I can be and all I can do now that I've got a chance to prove myself. Destiny, self-determination or pure dumb luck, I don't know which of them to thank for the way things played out for me today, but I feel like I'm on the cusp of something huge and I'm *really* bloody excited.

CHAPTER EIGHT

My first day in my new job is everything I hoped it would be.

No. Correction, it's even better.

'Lesson one,' announces Colm as we stand at the taps. 'The ancient art of pulling the perfect pint of Guinness.' He places a cold empty pint glass at a slant to the nozzle of the tap and begins a slow, steady pour. 'Patience, you must have patience. Don't ever rush this. Ever.' We wait, with patience. 'Leave two fingers' width of space from the top.' He settles the pint on the counter and folds his arms. 'Now we wait again. We'll be back in good time to put a head on it, and only then is it ready to go out to the customer.'

We wait. Both of us arms crossed, transfixed by the swirl and settle of the ashen storm in a pint glass, lost in it, oblivious to anything else for a couple of moments.

'Now,' he says, just as the liquid darkens to pitch and stills. 'Now we're ready. The moment a perfect line settles between the creamy white and the black stuff. That's the moment to add the head. Press the tap backwards, just enough so it reaches the edge of the glass – no spilling over, but don't leave them short either.' I nod my understanding. I'm the apprentice here and I take every word as gospel. 'It's got to be right, Evelyn. In the pub trade in Dublin, there is an expectation, a standard that must be honoured. You can set the place on fire, you can have people sitting on boxes instead of chairs and get them to eat from their laps. They won't hold it against you. But serve them a bad pint and you're finished.'

'But what happens if you're really busy? You can't spend this amount of time every time someone orders a Guinness, right?'

Colm shakes his head. 'Even if you have a crowd ten deep, they'll have to wait. And they'll expect to wait, so don't fret about that. Get a name for serving a bad pint and your business is gone. Get a name for being the busiest place in town and you'll only get busier.'

He hands me the pint. 'There. Try that.'

When your boss makes you drink before lunchtime, you know you've found the best job in the world. I take a long, slow sip. It is delicious: cold, creamy, with a dark, roasted bite to it. I smile over the glass. I think of Rosie serving all her girls big, filling pints such as these. Savouring the taste of rebellion, licking off their white moustaches with devilment in their laughing eyes. What a great way to fight a cause.

'Worth the wait,' Colm concludes. 'Next up, how to change a barrel.'

And so my pub education continues. And I must say, after all my years of school, Colm Munroe is the best teacher I've ever met.

After a few days, I feel completely comfortable in my new role. Christy has kindly helped with my training by drinking any practice Guinness that I pour, giving me marks out of ten for each. My highest score is currently an eight, but that may be because he was half-cut by then. None the less, I'm glad to have somebody to test my new-found skills on. A few regulars toddled in mid-morning today and they've stayed in the snug drinking solidly, but other than that, the only customers have been a few tourists who came in to use the toilet then walked straight back out again. This place is a long way off being the busiest place in town.

I push open the pub door and step outside. The street is really busy, jam-packed with people walking in both directions. A good mix of locals carrying groceries, visitors hefting backpacks, office workers with briefcases and uni students with school bags and laptops. Why are all these people walking past us day after day? Our pub is perfectly located here on the corner of two major streets, the ideal meeting place for so much of this passing trade. As far as I can see in either direction, we have no competition. There are some cafés, a few restaurants, newsagents and a craft shop, but no other pub in the area. So why are we empty? Why is business so slow? I cross over to the other side of the street to gain some perspective, to view Rosie Munroe's from the outside in its entirety.

Right. I think I've got my answer.

The place looks like a scruffy tip. The paint is peeling, great chunks of plaster are missing and the upstairs windows are so dirty they look as if they've been painted in.

The sign itself is intact, but it's tired, as is the surrounding whitewash. The creeping ivy needs to be cut back and the front area needs a good sweep; crisp packets, takeaway trays and general street litter has collected under the picnic tables, giving it a grubby, neglected look.

But with a little bit of time and effort, it would be quite easy to fix. A cosmetic facelift, nothing structural. A power hose and a lick of varnish would see it transformed, gleaming even. And a gleaming pub serving the perfect Guinness at a major crossroads without any competition sounds like a very interesting project. I think of what Christy said, that this place could be a little gold mine; more than that, it could be a lifeline, a place of fun and sanctuary away from the pressures of daily living, a place where people could come to meet their friends, listen to music, offload their troubles and find a listening ear and an understanding smile.

When I walked into Rosie Munroe's just a few days ago, I felt that I was on the outside of my own life, trying to find a way in. One afternoon and the kindness of two old men with a willingness to hear me out changed all that. And even if I don't last beyond my trial, already I'm starting to consider things I wouldn't have done previously, not afraid to look further afield and move out of my comfort zone. I can pull a pint. I can change a barrel. I can hold my own in bantering with the regulars. Now I just need to get more people over the threshold, because once they are in, I know they'll love it just as much as I do.

I make a mental checklist of what needs doing. Resources are limited, so it's more elbow grease than a complete refit. But even small changes will send out a new message, make the place more inviting. I remember when I took over my classroom when I started at St Mary's. That was a tip as well. I thought to myself: how can I invite children here? How can I ask them to take pride in themselves and their work if they look around and their environment is dirty and unloved?

So I spent the last few days of the summer holidays stripping the walls of minging old posters and unhooking furry blue sandwiches from behind the radiators and scraping ancient chewing gum from under the desks. I painted every wall dazzling white, as if to say: *We are starting afresh. We are beginning with a clean slate.* And then I strung up some bunting and created colourful display boards of inspirational people and motivational quotes. With just a little time and effort, the space was transformed from a horrid, oppressive cell to a happy, thriving place where the kids loved to be.

Surely I can do the same with Rosie Munroe's? I know the scale is much greater, but in principle it's the same. I did it before, so I could definitely do it again. One thing is for sure, I couldn't make it look any worse.

I walk back in through the front door. I've gotten used to Colm now and I know he's not always up for change, so I'll have to approach this carefully. I want to help him, not tell him how things should be done. I slip into the snug, where he is poring over the newspaper. This is the perfect opportunity.

'Colm, you wouldn't mind if I did a bit of a tidy outside, would you? Wash down the windows, sweep up. Just a little spruce?'

Engrossed in the article he's reading, he doesn't even look up. 'Whatever you like, Evelyn. Sounds good.'

And that's all the permission I need.

Three hours, five sponges and a shitload of elbow grease later and the 'face' of Rosie Munroe's is gleaming. I throw a final bucket of hot sudsy water at the brickwork and painted wall to dilute the smell of all the bleach and vinegar I've used to remove the build-up of years of grime and dirt, greasy handprints and car fumes. It's a job well done.

With my jeans rolled up and my T-shirt sopping wet, I cross the road to take a look at the building, and I can't help but beam with pride and satisfaction at the difference. Now *this* looks like a pub people might want to spend some time in. I'm already thinking flower baskets, a chalkboard of daily specials, even a bowl and biscuits for passing dogs. Muffin would certainly approve of that. My hands are itching to get stuck in, to take this to the next level. This is only the beginning, I can feel it.

I watch a small group of office workers stop and look through the doorway. They pause a moment, then shrug, nod and step inside the pub. Looks like we've got some new customers already! A soft-faced lady from the café opposite steps out onto the pavement chatting to a red-haired man with a guitar strapped to his back, a takeaway coffee in his hand.

'Great job,' he says to me. 'I've been watching you scrub all day. Tell you what, you haven't half changed the look of the place; brightens up the whole street.'

'It's wonderful to see,' says the café lady. 'It's broken my heart watching her get so run-down.' She holds out her hand and introduces herself as Agnes. The guitarist holds out his hand too.

'I'm Danny. I play around here most days, so I might see you when I call in and have a pint with Colm.' As his eyes meet mine, I feel a sudden flutter in my stomach.

Ah, this must be the busker who sometimes helps Colm out. What a nice guy. What a nice, beautiful guy. I rub my wet, wrinkly palms down my thighs and shake his hand. 'I'm Evelyn. I just started, on trial, to see if Colm needs an extra pair of hands.' I find myself rambling a bit, a little jarred at how unexpectedly attractive I find him. Big dark-brown eyes, hair curling softly at his neck, and such a sweet, almost shy smile. Bloody hell, he is gorgeous. I feel a rash of heat burning its way to my cheeks as I realise that I look like a washerwoman, I smell like drains and my wet white T-shirt is completely see-through. I can only imagine that my face and hair resemble an early Picasso. That Picasso *himself* would have subsequently binned. I make my excuses and point back over the road. 'Drop in any time,' I tell him.

'Will do. Looks like Rosie Munroe's is back.' He smiles, his eyes crinkling at the corners, and disappears on his way.

I take out my phone and ask Agnes to snap a picture of me and the pub. It feels momentous somehow. This is something I want to remember, because right now, I feel absolutely ecstatic. I've got a sense that this is a breath of new life, a second wind, not only for this old pub but also for me.

Is Rosie Munroe's back?

I think it's been there all along somewhere, waiting for the right person, for the right time.

Just like me.

At the end of my trial week, Colm breaks the news. As a result of my 'little spruce' of the outside, footfall has increased by just enough to warrant me securing a full-time job on minimum wage. I'm staying on! I pinch both Colm's cheeks with my fingers and plant a kiss on his forehead. Christy creases up when Colm needs to take out his hanky to dab his poor damp forehead, his cheeks burning with embarrassment.

'Getting hot under the collar there, Colm? A kiss from a beautiful girl; you never lost it! Always one for the ladies,' he teases. Colm rolls his eyes, a reluctant smile playing on his lips, and tells Christy he's barred. And again, my two new old buddies nearly choke with laughter.

When I get home, I climb upstairs and knock on Moira's door as I do every night, trying to get hold of her to discuss whether she still wants me to tutor her granddaughter, but yet again, there's no answer. Maybe they regularly go out for a meal, or to a show, or for a walk, spending their evenings doing nice things together. This time, I scribble a note explaining that I've now got a full-time position at Rosie Munroe's, so if she wants me, it's probably best that she calls in to the pub and we can catch up there. If I'm honest with myself, I'm half hoping that she reneges on the arrangement. I'm going to be rushed off my feet at the rate the pub is going, and already I've noticed that dealing with Moira is far from straightforward. I try one last time – 'Moira? It's Evelyn here. Just hoping for a quick word?' – but nothing happens. So I shove my note under her darkened door, the only sound from the other side a screeching chorus of mewling cats, then, with my conscience clear that I've tried my best, race downstairs two steps at a time, bursting to tell Tara the wonderful news about my new job.

CHAPTER NINE

Almost on cue, the sound of a guitar floats across the street as I water the flowers and put out the new chalkboard. I don't want to admit to myself that I take a lot longer than I need to, straightening the picnic tables and moving ashtrays just so I can hear him, catch a glimpse of him on the other side of the road.

For the past two weeks now, every single day, Danny Foy the gorgeous guitarist has sat on an upturned wooden box outside Agnes's café, singing and strumming away. His voice is spectacular. Soft and deliberate when he finger-picks the heartfelt time-worn traditional love songs, my favourite being 'Caledonia'. The first time I heard him sing this, I had to hold my arms for goose bumps – such a sudden, overwhelmingly emotional response. Maybe it was the words reminding me of home, or maybe it was the memory of my own father singing this song as he tended the horses when I was little, but my eyes pricked and I had to swallow hard to hold in my tears. Despite the traffic and the relentless city din, I heard every note, every careful pluck of his strings.

But he doesn't just do traditional Irish songs. He's pretty unpredictable. His set changes with his mood. If there are tourists about, he'll bash out a spirited 'Wild Rover' or 'Whiskey in the Jar'; sometimes he plays alternative covers of pop songs. The hen and stag parties love this, laughing and dancing to a fun, folksy take on Britney or Abba. He has a gift for reading the crowd, tuning in to what they want to hear, what they need to hear. Yesterday a school group was walking towards him, two rows of five-year-olds in their little uniforms, holding hands, their knapsacks nearly as big as they were. He stopped what he was singing and started up 'Reach for the Stars', knocking his knees together in a funny little dance to make them smile. They gathered around him, clapping along, singing the chorus with him at the tops of their voices, their sweet splayed hands raised over their heads as they reached up to the sky. It was joyous. I grabbed a box of chocolate bars from the stock cupboard, ran across the street and handed one to each of them. 'This has been the highlight of the trip,' said the teacher. 'No museum visit can compete with a live performance and free chocolate.'

I can tell it's not just me that keeps a lookout for him. I've noticed a few other locals – Agnes from the café is a fan too, and Jimmy the grocer comes out to the front of his shop to listen when Danny's playing – but I don't think any of them are as loyal as I am. I am his number-one fan, no doubt about it. I don't know how anyone could hear these songs, hear his voice, the subtle chord changes, the gentleness of his strum, and not crave them day after day. But then again, I've always had a passion for music, so maybe I'm just a little more infatuated and excited by his sound than anyone else. I've played the harp for as long as I can remember, and piano and violin and trumpet. I can have a go on most instruments, to be honest. Even the didgeridoo that Tara brought me back from Australia. But I don't have the performance X-factor like he does. That's a real talent in itself, and he's got it in spades.

Now he finishes a fun, rowdy singalong of 'The Fields of Athenry' with a jolly bunch of football fans and then launches into something I haven't heard him play before. I've never heard this song anywhere before. I crouch down and busy myself at the chalkboard so I can buy more time to listen, hear what his new sound is all about. I watch how he's closed his eyes in deep concentration, and the way he's repeating the same chords makes me think he's composing this song right here on the spot. I like that I'm witnessing this, especially since, after just a few chords, the stripped-back acoustic feel and the tender plucking of his strings mean the song is already my new favourite.

I lean against the window box, rest my arms on the ledge and watch him, safe in the knowledge that whilst he's immersed in his composition, his eyes are shut and he can't see me. I can't tear myself away, though. Some tourists strolling by stop in their tracks, nodding their heads and widening their eyes before they take their phones out to record him. I don't blame them; anyone would want to watch how passionately this guy plays. The way he keeps his eyes closed the entire time, his long dark eyelashes fanning out in a beautiful crescent, focusing intently on every stroke against every string. He sits cross-legged with the guitar upright between his legs, and then he pulls it against his chest and plays it like a stand-up bass. It's mesmerising to behold, so much so that I catch myself holding my breath, and I don't even realise it until he plays the final note and I shudder, finally ready to exhale.

It doesn't help that he's remarkably good-looking. Not in a way that Tara might agree with – she likes slim, Latin-looking types with polished caramel skin and no hair on their bodies. No hair at all. Good luck finding one of them in Dublin. Danny has dark auburn hair and porcelain skin, with a smattering of freckles across his cheekbones. He's so different, and though I've barely spoken to him yet, I've watched and listened to him so often I feel like I know him already. And I really like what I see.

A slow grin spreads across his face, almost as if he can hear what I'm thinking. I blush and busy myself with the cloth in my hand, pretending to rub down the picnic benches. My cheeks are flaming red and I chastise myself: *Don't be ridiculous, Evelyn, how could he possibly hear your thoughts?* But I take a deep breath and turn to look at him again, just to make sure.

A few regulars start to straggle into the pub, so I follow them in and start the service for the day. I've made and put out some sandwiches on the counter, and I've written up the lunchtime specials – basically a cheese or bacon sarnie and a drink for a fiver, as our kitchen facilities are limited – on the chalkboard outside, along with a daily quote. Today's reads:

Roses are red. Bacon is yummy.
Poems are hard.
Bacon.

It is actually attracting the office crowd.

Inside, I've kitted the snug out with a selection of retro board games, as people seem to like a light game of Connect 4 with their lunch. I've rearranged the tables so they are in a horseshoe shape instead of isolated little islands. At the back I uncovered a pool table, which I dusted off, and now we've got some older school kids coming in during their lunch break. They play a few games over soft drinks, crisps and the odd sandwich, which all adds up.

But just as we seem to be taking flight and are steadily busy all day, Colm's health has deteriorated. Christy noticed that he seemed even more breathless and tired than normal and convinced him to go and see the doctor, telling him that he needn't worry about the place, it was in safe hands with me, so there was no excuse not to go. When he got there, the doctor referred him to the hospital to review his medication, amongst other things he wasn't so willing to divulge. He did tell us that he has to have surgery on his fingers so he'll be around a lot less, but this week I've hardly seen him at all. I've been rushed off my feet, but I don't want poor Colm to worry, so I've told him that it's all in hand and I can manage on my own until he comes back.

In a way, being so busy suits me. From the moment I wake up to the moment I creep into the flat and collapse into my sister's bed, I am fully alive, in the moment, thinking of nothing but what I am doing right here, right now. And that feels so liberating. Free from the regrets of the past and the pressures of the future. Just being here – just *being* – is more than enough.

The clock strikes midday and like clockwork in walks my favourite customer, Liz, with her long black coat, dark glasses and cropped silver hair. She takes her seat at the bar with the *Racing Post*, looking out through the sunlit stained-glass windows. As I hand her her usual half a lager, she taps her pen on the counter, looking confused.

'Are you all right today, Liz?' I ask her.

'As good as I can be, Evelyn. Hard to pick a winner these days.'

I turn her paper round to have a look, running my finger down the list. I stop on Leap of Faith. 'I'd go for that one.'

'Forty to one; he hasn't a chance.'

I shake my head. 'Don't look at the odds, look at the trainer. Jimmy O'Hara doesn't train horses to fall at the first hurdle.'

'And how would you know anything about Jimmy O'Hara?'

'My family had horses,' I tell her. 'We took care of them when they were injured or too old to race any more. My father liked the odd bet, and I guess I just picked it up.'

Liz circles Leap of Faith with her pen. 'Well, I think that's worth a flutter. Thank you very much, Evelyn, and if I win at these odds, you can be sure I'll be back in with a smile on my face and there'll be a drink in it for you.'

She raises her glass, lifting her light-grey eyes to mine across the bar. 'This place used to be packed, people lining up around the corner to get in every night of the week.' She points to the curtain pulled closed across the back part of the pub. 'It was the heart of the music scene here in Dublin. Old Rosie, the landlady, was a great music lover – launched loads of bands, musicians, singers, songwriters. You could come from anywhere, show up with an instrument or able to hold a tune, and you'd be guaranteed a place on the stage, an audience, a hot meal and a bed upstairs.'

'Wow. I had no idea.' I didn't even know there were rooms upstairs, never mind a stage. I look around and notice the elevated platform hidden behind stacks of spare chairs covered with a heavy dust sheet. I walk over with Liz and lift it up, dust flecks rising and dancing in the stained-glass-coloured sunlight. I cover my nose and Liz starts to cough, but before I fold the sheet down again, I notice the legs of a grand piano, and a guitar stand. 'What happened to this place? Why did it stop playing music?' I can't imagine how something so important, so vital, so promising could just fall apart and fade away.

Liz strolls back to her stool, swallowing the last of her lager down in one gulp. Her coughing stops. 'When Rosie died, everything ground to a halt. She was the one with all the contacts; she had a relationship with the bands, the agents. They'd always make room in their schedules to play here because they wouldn't want to let Rosie down. There's a lot more to running a pub than serving drinks. You need to be a people person. You need to be interested in humanity. In sharing in its highest and lowest points. A baby is born, a new job, a chance meeting with an old friend, what do we do? We share it over a drink. A sudden death, you lose your job, your home, your partner leaves you, what do we do? We share it over a drink. For most people, it's not about the alcohol. It's about the sharing, the connection. And if you can do that, if you can help those who need to share, you'll never be without business, because people's need for connection is never going to go out of fashion.'

She slides her paper over to me. 'Right, Evelyn, thank you for this little tip. I'm off to place a bet. Leap of Faith… I like the sound of it already.'

And so do I.

CHAPTER TEN

Quit talkin' and start chalkin'!
Pool table NOW OPEN!

I watch Danny for longer than I should as I write up my chalkboard. I've already helped Liz pick her horse, and prepared the bacon sarnies for the late-lunchtime rush. The sun is shining, so the door is open, and the spring sunlight floods in through the stained-glass panels of the windows. As I step back inside, the jewelled light dances around the high vaulted ceilings and roots me to the spot in utter awe. How beautiful to be in such a serene, warm space right in the middle of a busy crowded city. How surreal. How wonderful. As I revel in this lovely moment, I realise that I'm not the only one to be moved by the scene.

'I told Colm last night that the place looks tip-top. You're doing a great job here, Evelyn. Breathed a bit of life back into it,' says Christy.

Today is a day of service and smiles, and a steady stream of people walking through the door, laughter in the corners, and goodbyes with promises to return and spread the word that Rosie Munroe's is well worth a visit. Standing behind the bar, bathed in the midday sunlight and listening to the gentle wordless strumming across the street, I feel like I am exactly where I am supposed to be. And I am happy. Simple as that.

Then I hear shouting, angry voices and the snap of something breaking. A scuffle. A slap. Angrier shouting. All from the pool room. I run in as fast as I can to see a gang of school kids: three boys on one side holding a blonde-haired girl back from a very angry black-haired goth girl with a broken cue in her hand.

'Okay, time to move outside, please,' I tell them in my calmest voice, trying to keep the situation measured. I know from school playground fights that the best thing to do is to try and de-escalate the situation and get them away from each other. However, in a school playground I'd have backup. I'd know their names. And I'd have some kind of authority: I could threaten to tell their parents, or suspend them. Here I've got nothing to back me up. And I don't know what these kids are capable of.

The goth girl darts me a look and then vaults over the pool table, reaching out for the blonde, who I notice is wearing a different school uniform. She grabs her by the neck and forces her backwards onto the floor. The gargling blonde's knuckles curl around the edge of the pool table in resistance, her face twisting with pain. The two of them spiral to the ground, each grasping a fistful of hair. At least ten boys are now gathered round, chanting, 'FIGHT! FIGHT! FIGHT!'

Holy shit. This is getting out of hand way too quickly. Serving drinks? Yes. Scrubbing toilets? Yes. Dealing with barroom brawls? No.

I look to Christy, who clenches his jaw and points at the door. 'I'll go and get help.' But as I look at the mob of boys, who are circling the two brawlers to create a boxing ring in the middle of the pool room, I know there's no time. This could escalate to a level of real danger very quickly – I have my eye on the broken pool cue, which could leave someone seriously hurt.

A scream from the centre of the tussle silences the crowd. I see some of the boys slide out their phones and start filming. There's no time to wait for help to arrive. Colm isn't here, and there's no way I can let this go any further while he's had such faith in me to do this job in the first place. It's now or never.

I grab hold of the goth girl by her shirt collar and drag her off the thrashing blonde's body. As I pull her away, she lashes backwards, and her fist hits me in the mouth. She stumbles back, pumping her shoulders up and down, sucking in short breaths through pouted lips. There is a smear of blood by her nose and her black hair is mussed up like candyfloss. I taste the metallic tang of blood in my mouth and realise that it's me that's bleeding. I reach out to steady the goth girl.

'Don't you touch me!' She holds a gold-ringed knuckle up to my face and then, eyes down, stomps past, smacking the door frame as she leaves. *Don't crack, Evelyn, don't fall apart. Be strong. Stay strong.*

'Okay, okay. Everything's okay now,' I hear myself say as I step back and let her leave. I stand stunned in the middle of the floor, my heart beating at a million miles an hour.

Then I hear a man's voice directed at the rest of the kids: firm, confident, young – not Christy or Colm. 'Out! Go on – all of you. You shouldn't even be here. Go back to school before I report the lot of you.' It's Danny. He spins around, walks towards me and places both hands on my shoulders, leaning in to study me closely. 'Feckin' hell, Evelyn, are you all right?' His eyes are so brown. Deep, dark chocolate brown.

'I am now, thanks,' I tell him.

'Let's get you some ice for that lip. Looks busted to me.' I run my tongue over my top lip and feel a huge hot lump. 'But don't worry, you're still a proper stunner. And this pouty lip thing is in vogue, I hear, so it's not all bad.'

I need to sit down. I need to get some air. He helps me to the bar and sits me on a stool. 'Just wait there. Don't move.'

There's not a chance of that; my head is ringing and I can feel my lip starting to really sting. Christy's moved to the doorway to make sure the kids don't return and is shaking his head. 'Flamin' kids. They should be doing something constructive, not hanging about in a pub in the middle of the day, only looking up from their gadgets to fight each other. I'm telling you, in my day it was altogether different. We were up to all sorts; girls had no time for fighting, too busy having the time of their lives. The sixties, that was the time to be young.' He pops a shot of whiskey in front of me. 'Drink this. For your nerves.'

I do as I'm told. I wince as I sip, as the alcohol stings my bust lip. Christy winces with me and puts a straw in the glass.

'There you are. That'll help, trust me.'

Funny thing is, I do trust him, so I take another sip.

Danny comes back with a first-aid kit and dabs my lip with antiseptic. 'They'll not mess with you again when they see you like this. I'm half afraid of you myself.'

I try to laugh, but it hurts.

He tells me to wait a second while he walks around the bar to the sink and opens a few drawers until he finds a clean dishcloth. He wets it under the tap, turns around and motions me over. 'Come here under the light so I can see it properly.' I do as he says, leaning into him under one of the low-hanging lamps. I balance on my elbows on the counter, my gaze to the ceiling. He takes my chin and angles my face to the left, pressing the cloth to my skin to clean off the drying blood. I wince. I didn't even realise how much it was hurting till he touched it.

He removes the cloth, rinses the blood from it under the tap and puts it back on my mouth, this time with an ice cube to numb the pain and bring down the swelling. He takes my hand and presses the ice wrap gently to my lip, letting me know exactly where to keep it.

My cheeks instantly heat from embarrassment. He is so close I can breathe in his scent. He smells lovely, a mixture of soap and leather. And I must look absolutely ridiculous like this, with a bloody face and a fat lip. I swallow, unable to speak for a moment, realising that it matters to me what he thinks of me, how he sees me.

I take a deep breath. The fight is barely registering with me now. It's like a little blip, I'm already over it; the big event is happening right this second. It's happening centimetres in front of my face, so close I can feel his actual breath as he checks my injuries. I can see each eyelash, each micro-movement of his face, his expression. His skin is soft and clear, his eyes so dark in contrast, focused on me, so close… It's doing nothing to slow down my heart rate.

'You seem to be quite the paramedic,' I say, my words muffled by my bulging lip and the icy cloth.

He cocks an eyebrow and a wicked little grin plays on his lips. He looks out of the window and then back to me. 'Me and my brother… when we were younger, we were always scrapping. Loved winding up the older kids, you know. We were cocky little shits, sure as anything that we could outrun them, and mostly we did, but there were a few times…' He points to a scar over his right eyebrow, then one across his knuckles and another directly under his chin. 'Sometimes we bit off more than we could chew, and let's say they caught up with us.'

'Siblings, eh? The only enemy you can't live without,' I say, and he nods thoughtfully. I like that.

'You're from the country, right? So you probably have forty brothers and sisters and the whole town is your extended family.'

I give him a withering look. 'Why is it that Dubliners have this idea that everyone outside of the capital is a hillbilly? That all we do is eat sackloads of potatoes and ride like rabbits all day?'

'Ride like rabbits? I didn't know that. Maybe it's worth a trip, in that case. So how many million siblings have you got?'

'Just one younger sister actually, Tara. I'm staying with her at the moment.'

'You get on?'

'Yeah, always. We are very different but we look out for each other.'

'Different?' Danny asks.

'She's taller, darker… more adventurous. She's much braver than me. Does her own thing.'

'You don't do your own thing?'

'Don't really know what my thing is yet; guess that's why I'm here. Trying to figure it out.'

He nods, holding my gaze thoughtfully, searching my eyes a beat too long.

'I like people who try.'

What is that supposed to mean? Is it a philosophical nugget, or something more? I look to the floor, trying to compose my thoughts.

He dabs my lip with the antiseptic one more time. 'Looking good,' he says, glancing straight at me. 'Even with a busted face.' He laughs. 'C'mon, let me walk you home.'

I hold up my hands. 'No thanks. I've got to stay here and work the bar; I'm not finished until this evening.'

'You serious? No offence, but most people'd throw in the towel after what just happened.'

I smile to myself. 'Yes, well, I must have some sticking power.'

Danny winks over to Christy. 'Well, looks like Evelyn'll be hanging around for another while yet. These country girls are tough.'

Christy swirls his drink around in the glass and holds it up in a toast to me. 'Good on you, Evelyn! Stand your ground. They'll not scare you off. But I'm going to tell Colm that you need an extra pair of hands in here; you can't do all this by yourself. Leave it with me.'

Does that mean Colm won't be back in full work mode for a while? If that's the case, a bit of part-time help with clearing up and keeping the place ticking over would be fantastic.

Danny slings his guitar on his back, writes his phone number on a beer mat and slides it over the counter to me. 'Call me when your shift is over and I'll come back to walk you home.'

'Honestly, there's no need. I'll be fine.'

He shoots me a wary look. 'Listen here, it's not you I'm worried about. This is a respectable area – can't have you wandering around these streets with your big fat lip, scaring children and tearing the shirts off teenagers.' He taps the beer mat. 'Call me. I want to walk you home.'

I shake my head. Can you imagine what people would think? Newly divorced Evelyn Dooley, black and blue from a brawl, spotted walking home from a pub with a strange man. If things were different, would I take him up on his offer? Absolutely. If I wasn't fresh out of a failed marriage and suspect that this is what they mean by a rebound romance? Absolutely. If I didn't care what people thought and was truly brave enough to take the next steps without fear of being hurt all over again? Absolutely.

But things are not that way for me yet. This little matter of a decree absolute is still very raw to me. I don't want to make another mistake. I don't want this to go any further. Because he is very much the kind of man I could fall in love with a little too quickly. And when it all goes pear-shaped, he is very much the kind of man that would absolutely annihilate my heart. So nope. I'm back on my feet, I'm happy, I'm doing well. I can't risk throwing all that away and messing up my life with another failed relationship. There's too much at stake, too much to lose, too much for my fragile heart. I can see by the glimmer in his eye that he's flirting with me. I need to set him straight.

'Look, Danny, I appreciate it, all your help today. But I'm just out of a relationship and the last thing I want is to start another one. Just so you don't waste your time, I'm not looking for anything with anyone right now.'

He pauses a moment, bites his lip, considers the beer mat and leaves it on the counter. 'As you like.' He slings his guitar over his shoulder, and when he reaches the door, he turns around. 'Good luck with all the stuff you're trying for. I hope you figure it out. And if you do change your mind, you have my number.'

My stomach folds in on itself. I have either done myself the biggest favour or the biggest disservice of my life. Attraction, the first flutters of possibility, the skin-tingling effect of someone standing close, someone you've watched from afar and tried not to daydream about. This wasn't something I was expecting to feel just yet. I've been so focused on getting my own life off the ground, I didn't factor in anybody else. I guess I thought that if I ever started seeing someone again, it would be a conscious, formal decision. A rational choice. Not just something that happened out of the blue and without my bidding. When I started on this journey, falling for another man was not something I'd worked into my plans. This excitement, this stirring in my chest was definitely not something I expected to feel right now.

But despite what I said to Danny and echoed to my heart about not wanting anything more, I slip the beer mat into my bag.

CHAPTER ELEVEN

I run my tongue over my hot fat lip for the hundredth time. I must be in shock. How the hell did the day turn out like this?

As I lock up the pub and make my way home, my phone vibrates in my pocket. I glance at it quickly, hoping it's Tara so I can fill her in on everything that's happened. With the time-zone difference and her crazy shift work, we are constantly missing each other. But it's not Tara. It's Mum. I swallow hard. I need to take this, as I haven't called her properly since arriving here a fortnight ago, which means I still need to break the news to her that I am no longer teaching, but working in a pub.

'How's the flat? How's the weather? How's Tara? How's work?' She launches in with the interrogation as soon as I answer.

'Brilliant. Everything is brilliant,' I tell her as I carefully move the phone away from the injured side of my face. 'I'm really enjoying it all.' And that's true. Even in spite of today. The work is hard, the clientele can be unpredictable, the shifts are long – sometimes a full twelve hours – but it's actually exactly what I need right now. I look forward to going in each day, to stacking the shelves and watering the flowers and prepping the sandwiches and then opening the doors and listening to Danny. Each morning I feel full of expectation and excitement as to what will happen and who will walk in next. Because you never know – and for the first time in my life, I'm okay with not knowing. Even a teensy bit exhilarated by not knowing. I might even uncover that stage tomorrow, see what kind of condition it's in. Who knows?

My mother relaxes her tone. 'Well at least that's something. I met Mrs O'Driscoll yesterday. She asked if you're teaching up in Dublin yet because no one has called for a reference. I told her you were, that you got a job the day after you arrived. She wants to know the name of the school, see if she knows anyone who could help you along.'

What a busybody! She has no intention of helping me along. More like ringing them up and telling them I'll poison their ethos. That I took a vow to be Mrs O'Connor for life and she'll make it her personal vocation to see that I do. I came up here to escape all that. Even if I was in a school, I wouldn't want her to have any chance of gossiping about me.

'Right… well the thing is, Mum, I'm not working in a school just yet. It'll take another couple of weeks until I know about anything available on that front, so just tell her I've gone into industry.'

'Oh? That sounds interesting. And what's that when it's at home?'

'I'm working in a pub.'

'For God's sake, Evelyn, are you trying to kill me altogether? Tell me you're pulling my leg – a pub! That can't be a good thing. If it was Tara that had turned her life on its head I'd be more prepared, I'd half expect it…'

I hold the phone away from my ear. If my dad was alive, he'd take over now and calm the whole thing down and make me feel better. Make my mum feel better. But of course he's not. And as hard as I tried to take his place and keep Mum happy and content, it wasn't something I really succeeded in. Yes, I stuck around, made sure she didn't feel alone. But that's what I'm realising. *Being* alone and *feeling* alone are two different things. With Tara and her flatmate away most of the time, I've been on my own more in the past couple of weeks than I have since… well, ever. I always imagined that being by myself would be lonely, that the emptiness, the silence would dissolve me, but I'm not finding that to be the case at all. I'm grand. If I'm not at the pub, I read and sing along to my favourite music and eat and rest and bathe and do as I please. I've not been lonely or bored once. I actually can't believe that this was something I was scared of; it was a completely irrational and unfounded fear. And possibly a fear that drove me to getting married earlier and staying married longer than was good for me.

'… She always had a reckless streak, but *you*! Evelyn, what on earth has gotten into you?'

I don't argue, I let her rant – she needs the release. I understand that she's trying to knock sense into me, that what I'm doing must seem to her like moving backwards, sinking downwards.

But here's the thing, I don't feel like I am.

I feel lighter, higher and happier than I have done in ages. I feel like I'm finally getting to know myself, as weird as that sounds. When I was with James, there were really only two things that happened in order to do anything, decide on anything: we'd either have to compromise or fight. And it's easy to forget what you actually like or want to do yourself – without consulting anyone – when you're always either compromising or fighting. Right now, I really like this new-found peace, this independence. I like my life. I'm not full of dread or despair or anger. I don't know what tomorrow will bring, but I've had a great today. I feel like I've *lived* today, like I'm starting to let myself be myself. I did it with fear. With pain. With doubt. With hands shaking and voice trembling… but I started. I've got a fat lip and Danny's number on a beer mat to show for it. And that feels good. That feels like I've lived. And that's not something I'm about to take for granted.

I stop walking, as I think I can hear Muffin whimpering in the background. *I miss you too, Muffin!* I step in from the footpath, away from the busy late-night traffic, so I can listen more closely.

'… Six months ago you had a fine family house, a husband and a respectable job, and you've thrown it all away – for what? To sleep on your sister's floor with a Mickey Mouse bar job. You gave up your marriage, your *life* for that? Enough of this nonsense. Just come back home, Evelyn. Now, this minute. Pack your bags and start your journey back to where you belong.'

A siren passing makes it difficult for me to hear what she is saying.

'… waste… disaster… out of your depth… from bad to worse…'

As bad as I feel that Mum is upset with me, I don't agree. I think my life is moving from bad to better. I need to give her a sense of how this is exactly the right thing for me now, so that she sees I'm doing okay and can stop worrying. I put her on speakerphone for a minute and text her the photo Agnes took.

'This is me outside Rosie Munroe's.'

'Well, you look…' There's silence for a moment; this is the first time my mother has paused to take a breath. 'I have to say that you look happy, delighted even. There's a healthy flush to your cheeks and you look better than I've seen you in a long time.'

'I *am* happy, Mum. The owner has given me lots of freedom, so I've taken it on as a little project, a challenge to myself to see if I can grow the business. I've started on the outside and I'm working my way in! You'll have to come up and visit. It's the real deal: original fireplace and flooring, the kind of place you walk in and immediately feel relaxed and welcome. I think you'll love it, Mum.'

'Well, if you're sure, Evelyn. If you're happy, then I'm happy. I'll tell that Mrs O'Driscoll that you're doing great. And by the look on your face in that photo, it seems you are.'

Good. I'm happy with that. I don't want her worrying herself into a frenzy. I think if she saw the place herself she'd fall in love with it too.

'Send me some more pics. I enjoy seeing what you're up to.'

I'm standing on the pavement outside our house now. 'No problem! I'll send some tomorrow. I've got to go now, Mum. I'm doing well, I promise. Give Muffin a treat from me,' I add.

And we kiss our goodbyes across the invisible network that connects us from one side of the country to the other, across all the fields and hills and rivers and lakes that lie in between Ballybeg and here.

I turn to go in through our gate, and what I see ahead of me momentarily roots me to the spot. I take a deep breath and squint forward, just to make sure that I've got this right.

Sprawled on the steps like a horrible black spider is the goth girl from the pub. Waiting on the steps of *our* house. Waiting for what? For me? It can't be… How could she have followed me home if she is here before me? I relax at the thought. It's a coincidence, nothing more. Maybe she's visiting someone. There is a studio flat on the top floor; I don't know who lives up there. Maybe she's waiting for someone. Maybe she can get a better signal for her phone here. I have no idea. The only thing I *don't* want her to be here for is me. I touch my fat lip. She can certainly pack a punch. This is actually the first time in my life I've ever been hit. At all.

I swallow hard, slowly lift the latch of the gate and brace myself for whatever is going to happen next. She's a teenager; from what I saw today, a sad and troubled teenager. Not someone to run from, but someone who needs help.

Her legs are stretched out in front of her and she is leaning with her back propped up against the railings. Her chin is tucked into her chest and she's muttering lyrics to the music I can hear coming from her headphones. The blue light of her phone illuminates her face.

'Hello?' I venture. 'Can I help you?'

She shifts inside her baggy black hoody, and her charm bracelets clatter as she lifts her head towards the sound of my voice. She sweeps back a mass of dark hair from her squinting eyes, then drops her head again.

'Excuse me,' I say. My voice is just above a whisper.

She doesn't move.

I lift my leg over her and try to step across her. 'Sorry, but I need to get in.'

She shifts again, and then slowly lifts her head to stare straight at my legs. Her eyes meet my knees, and her forehead furrows as she leans forward with a deep scowl on her face. She lifts a hand and pokes my knee with her finger, almost as if she's never seen a knee before. She starts to giggle, high-pitched and dreamy, then she lolls her head backwards and her eyes roll back. And that's when I realise that's she's pretty pissed. I fold down on my knees and start pinching her face.

'Hello? Hello? Can you talk to me? What's your name?'

'Roo,' is all she can manage, her voice slurred and loose.

Is she drunk? Or drugged? I'm hoping just drunk. I move closer. I can definitely smell spirits – brandy, I think. Please, God, let it just be alcohol…

I turn her onto her side to try and get her standing, and she pukes down the steps by my feet. Which is a good sign: whatever poison is in her stomach is ejecting itself.

I bang on the door. No tentative knocking and waiting at a time like this; none of Moira's avoidance tricks, hiding inside. 'MOIRA! Come out here! I need you, it's an emergency!'

I hear the shuffle of feet on the landing, along with some belligerent muttering, then the sound of the latch lifting on the inside, and Moira, dressed in a satin kimono with a full face of powdery make-up, appears in the doorway. She eyes me curiously for a second, probably wondering why I haven't used my key, then glances behind her.

'I've got company,' she tells me in a firm whisper and wide fuck-off eyes.

I ignore her. 'I need your help,' I say. She slides her glasses down from her head, opens the door further and grimaces at me before darting her gaze down to the shivering black ball at my feet. Her eyes widen.

'For God's sake, Ruby, what the hell have you done to yourself now?' She grunts with irritation.

I thought goth girl was just some crashed-out teenager who couldn't make it home, but Moira is acting like she knows this kid. Like she's seen it all before and this is a regular occurrence.

'Do you know who she is?' I ask.

Moira folds her arms over her chest. 'I'll say. She's my bloody granddaughter.'

CHAPTER TWELVE

Once we get inside, we push Ruby and her jelly-like legs up the stairs, then steer her straight into Moira's bathroom.

'Nearly there now, you're doing so well.' I stroke the girl's back as she retches over the toilet bowl. We establish that she's not taken any drugs and I feel a huge wave of relief wash over me. Drink we can help with; anything more would need an ambulance. Somewhere in the background, I can hear Moira ushering her gentleman caller out the front door. It's a wise move; it's pretty difficult to conduct a romantic affair to the guttural soundtrack of teenage vomiting.

Once Ruby seems to have completely emptied herself of brandy and spaghetti hoops, we lay her down on the bathroom floor, gently propping her head up with a cushion. She shivers, shudders momentarily, a reaction to the shock that her body is experiencing.

'Moira, we need more towels – blankets will be too heavy; can you get me four towels?' I ask, and Moira opens the hot press and takes them out, draping them on her granddaughter's limbs and torso one by one. The shivering subsides. Ruby raises her hand above her face, feeling the space in front of her.

'Where am I?' Her voice is breathy and ragged, a hoarse whisper. I watch her body relax and loosen. Her eyes open slightly, red-rimmed and glassy. She is squinting at the light bulb above her. 'Why are we here?' She touches her hair, grabbing bunches as if feeling for knots.

'It's okay, you're safe. It's all okay. You're at your nan's place. You drank too much, but you've been sick so you'll feel better soon.'

Moira tuts and leaves the bathroom, and a few seconds later I hear the front door shut. Looks like she's left us to it. Ruby sits up and I wrap more towels tightly around her shoulders, then offer her a glass of water. She brings it to her lips and slugs it back. I get her another – she does the same again. She is running on empty, this poor girl; there's nothing left inside her. She turns weakly and points a finger at me.

'Why do I know you?'

'I'm Evelyn. I'm staying downstairs with my sister Tara.'

'Tara and Inez?'

I nod.

'They're cool.' She winces. She's going to have a belting hangover after this. 'Do you work at the pub?'

'That's right.' I try to smile at her so she knows I'm okay about earlier.

'Your lip looks like it's split.' She squeezes her eyes shut again and pinches her nose, as if trying to stem a memory. Or tears.

I shrug. 'Don't worry about that, Ruby, it's you we're taking care of now.'

I turn on both taps and start to run a bath. 'Right, you hop in and get yourself cleaned up. You'll feel a million times better afterwards. I'll make some tea and toast. That always works. I'll stick your stuff in the wash and you'll be right as rain in no time.'

I gather up her hoody and the towels. She reaches for the edge of the bath to lift herself up, and I support her by the elbow. She looks fragile and pale; she's definitely going to need something in her stomach. 'Butter and jam, or toasted cheese?'

'Don't mind.' She shrugs.

'I'll do both.'

I hover, ready to steady her. But she's managed to get up and is on her feet now, a flush of pink dappling her cheeks and the faintest of smiles on her lips. She looks up at me and inhales a calming breath, then mouths the words *thank you*.

Satisfied that she can manage, I make my way to Moira's kitchen and start raiding the cupboards. There is barely anything in them beyond cans of spaghetti hoops. Same with the fridge. Half-open cans of spaghetti hoops. I'm well aware that it's not my place to go poking my nose in, but I did notice Moira's reaction... because there really wasn't one. I can't believe she'd just walk out on her granddaughter like that. I get that she is angry – my mother would go crazy if either of us turned up this drunk and puked on the stairs, but she'd never just *leave* us. She'd take care of us until we were well enough to get the robust bollocking that would no doubt come our way. This just makes me feel even sadder for Ruby and her situation. From the pool table incident it appears she doesn't get on with her peers, and by the looks of this she doesn't get on with her nan either. That's pretty much your whole world when you're a teenager.

I call in a pizza delivery, as I'm not comfortable going through Moira's stuff and she's nowhere to be seen. Ruby definitely needs some looking after. Moira mentioned that she was seventeen, but still, she's not ready to face the world all by herself. Considering the girl's clothes all have a sour sick smell, I have little choice but to load the washing machine as well. If Moira has a problem with that, so be it. It's out of the question to leave Ruby here by herself in this state, in this mess, without anyone to help her or any food to eat. I empty her pockets before I put her clothes in the machine: no money, just a tissue, some earbuds, a bus card – and a crumpled-up letter.

I hear Ruby turn off the bath taps and splash into the water. Should I read the letter? The concerned teacher in me says yes, absolutely – it might give me some insight into what's going on with this poor girl. Who is Ruby? Is there something I can do for her? The nosy barmaid in me also says yes, one hundred per cent. I'm the only one here and I need to know what on earth is going on.

The balled-up paper is regular lined A4. The writing is smudgy, in blunt pencil. I try to iron the page out with my hand and make out the distressed handwriting – if I found this in a school, I'd immediately associate it with a kid in need and try to get to the bottom of it, try to figure out where the problem lies – home, school, peers? In a way, I am Ruby's teacher, as Moira asked me to be her tutor, so that gives me a professional duty to find out as much as I can in order to help. This lost girl punches classmates in pubs at lunchtime and gets slaughtered on her own only to come back to an empty house. I need to know more.

I glance over my shoulder one more time to make sure I'm alone and then begin to read.

Deer Nan,

I dunno waht makes me anser back at you.

I need to get out. i always leave at the rong tmie anb make thngs even worse. then I try to befend myself and get into deeper trudle! I rilly try hard not to get into so mcuh trudle but it awlays hpauns. this is going to snoud well stuquid but I don't want to be me anymroe. I cant spell as well as my frens or read as good. in fcat I htae reabing altogether it's the wrost thing ever. The teechers are triyng to work on it with me but they are to bisy to do anthin about it.

I wish one day smoetihng wud take it all away. I'd do a swap in my persnoalty fro me to be gud and us to get on. im sik of not bein as goob as evry one else in the wrold. I hjust wnt to draw and paint and foget all abut exams and scool. I hate scool so mch.

its mus be rilly anoyin havin me as ur grandawter geting things the rong way round and messin up the hoel time.

I don't want to be stuk in this hoel. Im onistley sacreb of how meen and sad and angry I feel cos when I do cok up I think ther is no one ther to ctach me so I just keep falling, I keep arguing, tahts the way ive awalys bin and I dnot spose ill change. one day I garentee im gona blow up and do sumtin stuqid over this.

Just wantd to get it of my chest strat away so we can make up qiukly and work on bein better at takin care of echother. onse yu've red this come finb me if you want, just tell me you get it, what im about.

Ruby x

I sink into the kitchen chair and try to process what I've just read. Where should I begin? *How* should I begin?

I fold up Ruby's letter and place it on the sideboard with the rest of her things. I remember what it feels like to be that young and feel that lost. To feel like nothing is ever going to work out the way you want it, the confusion with a world that seems chaotic and conflicting and cruel. But I was lucky. For a big part of my childhood, I still had my lovely dad, who would listen to me and talk through things and sit with me at the dining-room table until I'd learnt my spellings or figured out long division or could name all the rivers and mountain ranges in Europe. It wasn't about the work really; it was about feeling hopeful, that we were working towards something, that I had a future and it was going to be bright and exciting and meaningful.

I look around Moira's flat and realise that it's not easy here for either of them. Whatever circumstance has brought them together – with at least forty years' gap between them – they could do with some help. I think I'm starting to get it, to understand what it is all about. And I think I know how I might make this a little better.

I agreed that I would be Ruby's tutor. That I would help her with whatever she needed. I'll keep my promise, not because I have to, but because I want to. I want to make things a little better for her, bring some of that hope back into her world. Looks like now is as good a time as any to begin.

I collect the pizza and plonk the box in the middle of the coffee table. I glance over at Ruby on the sofa, her head against the armrest, chewing on her bottom lip and squinting as if she's trying to solve some painful puzzle. Boyfriend trouble? Parent trouble? Money? Relationships? Future? I think about how my problems and Ruby's are probably very similar, despite the age gap between us.

'Dig in! This smells amazing.' I slide onto the couch beside her and lift an oozy pizza slice to my mouth. 'Please eat as much as you want. If you don't help me, I might scoff the lot.'

Ruby turns around and shifts up in her seat, taking a slice. And then another, and another, until the colour starts coming back into her cheeks and she seems to have regained some energy. We drink pints of water and chat about our favourite food, the best pizzas we've ever had, the worst. She's a great kid. Chatty and engaging. We're midway through discussing the merits of a stuffed crust when she reaches under the coffee table and slides a large black folder from the bottom shelf, resting it on her lap.

'Thank God it's here,' she says. 'I've been searching for this all week.' She tightens her hold on it, an obvious wave of relief washing over her dark features.

'School work?' I venture.

'Yeah, some of my art exam prep. I love art. I want to do it all the time; it's the only reason I even turn up at school.

'What do you like the best?'

'Portraits,' she says, her eyes flashing with excitement. 'I love drawing people, especially faces.'

'Is that what's in there?'

She nods.

'You don't have to show me, but I'd love to take a look.'

Ruby pauses and rubs her hand across her neck. 'Okay, but this isn't my finished work. Some bits I've really messed up, so it's not as I want it yet. It's actually really embarrassing…'

She hands me the portfolio and I lift the cover, struck by the intensity of the eyes staring back at me. It's a close-up of a female face, a modern-day Mona Lisa – a snapshot like she is running, looking back momentarily. Her eyes are fearful but defiant, like she has accepted the threat and is now gauging her chances of survival.

'Wow, Ruby, you're full of surprises – this is great, I love the idea. We're so used to seeing Mona Lisa frozen in time, still and almost lifeless, and here she is alive and contemporary, hooped earrings, cherry lips, smoky kohl eyes. I've been to a few galleries in my time and I would stop to take this in. I'm serious, I love it.'

'My art teacher says I've overworked it.' She points towards the temples, under the eyes and the cheekbones. 'I should have stopped but I kept adding more and more, and well, less is more so I can't use it as my exam piece now.'

As I lean in close to the portrait, studying the texture of the paint, I have an idea. I root around in my bag and take out a tiny make-up palette. I've watched Tara transform herself from a bleary-eyed, yawning bedhead to a flawlessly glamorous stewardess enough times to know my way around the camouflaging tricks disguising everything from hangovers to jet lag

'I think I can salvage this, you know – what do you think, shall I give it a go?'

She raises a perplexed eyebrow.

'You trust me?'

Ruby nods. 'You can't make things any worse.'

With my little finger, I start by dabbing concealer under Mona Lisa's eyes, restoring the flattened matte effect. I continue gently dabbing and smudging all over the left side of the face, using a bronzing blend to darken the natural hollows until the dimension comes back and the depth is regained. To finish, I brush an arc of highlighter along the brow bone, and that is it – Mona Lisa back from the dead.

I hold it at arm's length underneath Moira's tasselled lampshade to give Ruby a clearer view.

'Holy shit. That is amazing. I mean, you've just saved me like forty hours' work.'

I remember another handy Tara tip and rummage around in my bag again for a mini can of hairspray. 'This will set it, seal it and give it a sheen.' I spray the refreshed Mona Lisa and hand the painting back to Ruby. 'All fixed!'

Ruby's chest puffs out and she lets out a huge sigh, examining the image and shaking her head. 'Thanks, Evelyn, this is great. Just a pity everything else can't be fixed so easily, right?'

I stay quiet, unsure of what to say. Ruby's hand strays back to her hair, her fingers scratching behind her ear.

'Sorry. I don't even know why I said that. Nobody wants to hear about someone else's problems.'

For a moment we both sit in silence, the weight of her words hanging in the space between us. Then I turn to her and place my hand gently on top of her folder.

'That's not the case, Ruby. You can tell me if there's something bothering you.'

She pauses for a moment before it all comes pouring out. 'I hate school so much. I just need to pass my art exam and I can do a foundation course next year. Nan doesn't want me to do it, she thinks it's a pointless course that's a waste of time and money.'

I listen as she describes the tension, the difficulty in going against other people's wishes when they think they know what's best for you.

'I would encourage you to be as honest as possible,' I tell her. 'Try to help her understand why it's so important to you. I know that's easier said than done; even at my age, I'm not always so good at being honest with my mother.'

Ruby sits up and crosses her legs on the couch, searching my face, concentrating on every word. She doesn't interrupt or dismiss anything I've said, which is quite unusual for a teenager at odds with the world. I can see so much despair in her eyes, but also a real desire, a determination to find a way out, to learn and listen and try to gather enough crumbs of advice to help her on her way.

'Ruby, I know all about putting the dreams of other people ahead of your own, and it makes perfect sense, because you don't want to let them down. You get worn down constantly arguing, fighting, so much so that you may even start to believe that your dream was a stupid idea in the first place. But giving in and doing what other people want you to do, that's not even the hard part.'

I swallow and realise something that I haven't seen so clearly before. 'The hard part comes afterwards. The hard part is keeping it up, trying to live that dream – that dream that isn't yours – convincingly over years and years and years. Ultimately, we can't: it's unsustainable, it's too hard over too long. If we could all pretend that well, then we'd all be Oscar winners.

'So what should I do?' she asks me, her eyes glassy with intensity.

'I can't tell you that, Ruby. That's one for you to figure out. But it's not as hard as it seems; I bet you already know deep down what you should do. No one expects you to make perfect choices, but if you make a mistake, let the mistake be *yours*, because then the lesson will make sense to you. If you make a mistake because of pressure from somebody else, you don't come away with a lesson, you come away with anger and blame.'

We both reach for another slice of pizza and settle back into Moira's tiger-print cushions. And as we munch away quietly, I realise that I'm not entirely sure which one of us I'm talking about any more.

CHAPTER THIRTEEN

He hasn't been outside at his usual time in his usual spot on the corner in almost a week. I've wanted to text him about it, just something bright and breezy. *Where are you? Missing the music... your music... missing your music and you.* No, I couldn't. That would come across wrong. If I do, it'll seem like I'm looking for something – which I am not. I'm positively not looking for something or someone. Even if it is someone like him. Even if it is *him*.

'Hey.' Ruby walks in through the pub door, her folder tucked under her arm. That must mean it's four o'clock. I've never known the day to go so fast. I used to yearn for the clock to strike four so I could take a moment to gather my thoughts, to have a quick coffee and freshen up before I was summoned to management meetings or parents' evenings or governor presentations or professional development workshops. It was never being with the kids, with the music that bothered me – I loved that, lived for it. But all the other stuff. That's what made me bite my nails to the knuckle and woke me up in the middle of the night, gasping for great big gulps of air as I'd dream I was being sucked under a giant wave. It happened so often that eventually James moved out into the spare room.

At least then I could stress myself out without the stress of stressing anyone else out. But not now. Now I sleep like a baby.

Ruby places her folder on the counter and pops up on to a bar stool beside Christy.

'How was school today?' I ask her.

'All right, actually.' She slides over her report card. *Distinction* is written at the top in green pen, with the comment *Well done, Ruby! Great concept, love the use of make-up as a medium, very post-modern.*

'I have never *ever* got a distinction before. And my teacher said this is a tough module and it sets me up nicely for my overall grade at the end of the course. So yeah, I'm chuffed.'

I crack open two bottles of sparkling water and we toast like it's a momentous victory. Because I think it is.

'Here's to you, Ruby, another step closer to your glittering future.'

'I'll drink to that,' she says.

Colm shouts his congratulations from the snug, where he's reading his paper, and Christy raises his glass too, applauding her.

'So what's today's homework then?' he asks.

'Art history.' She rolls her eyes. 'Boring. And not exactly my strong point.'

Christy straightens his back and feigns mock offence.

She shrugs. 'What? It's old news, it's gone, over with – nobody cares any more.'

He considers her point for a moment. 'You're right and you're wrong. Depends on the history – I agree that some things are best left in the past, but let's not get carried away. Read out what you've got to do.'

Ruby presses a nail-bitten finger to the small lettering and takes her time reading out each word as carefully as she can. '"Cultural heritage is…" I don't know what this says.'

Christy slides it over and bends down to take a closer look. '"Cultural heritage is the legacy of physical artefacts and the intangible attributes of a group or society inherited from past generations, maintained in the present and bestowed for the benefit of future generations. Cultural heritage includes tangible culture such as buildings, monuments…'

Ruby rolls her eyes. 'See? Doesn't even make sense.'

Christy beckons to her. 'Come and sit here and we'll have a think together. I have a few ideas that might do the trick.' He scans through the assignment. 'It says here you need to complete a five-minute multimedia presentation on the topic. You must include factual content, visual images and video, and conduct an interview.'

Ruby pokes two fingers down her throat in response. 'I hate history so much. And this teacher is a complete control freak. If it's not perfect, he'll fail me. He's like a robot – work, work, work... I'm definitely going to fail this one.' Her chest sinks, deflated.

'Evelyn, coffee over here, please. We've got some very important work to do.' Christy pulls his glasses down the bridge of his nose, grabs a pen from Ruby's pencil case and starts drafting their presentation.

And that's when I hear it. With a flutter in my chest at the idea, at the possibility, I hear the familiar opening strum, the seamless chord change, the voice – mellow and gentle, but crackling with hope, with despair, with something I just cannot put my finger on. But that I can't get out of my mind.

I move to the front bay window, hidden from Danny's sight, and close my eyes, searching the sound, searching that voice.

And then, mid song, it goes quiet. He stops. The silence hangs in the air as if someone has pulled a plug, or cut the note he was singing in half. What's happened? What's going on? Is he okay? I rush out of the door and on to the street outside.

He's still there. He nods at me with a grin, brown eyes dancing. Then he taps his guitar, shuffles his feet and starts to bounce up and down. He looks back down at the guitar, spins on his heel and starts strumming. It's a song I haven't heard him play before, but one I recognise...

'Come on Eve-lyn.' He throws back his head and starts singing with gusto.

I let out a huge breath. Until this moment, I didn't realise how much I'd missed him. A stag group gathers in around him, kicking up their legs like can-can dancers to the beat. 'Come on, Eve-lyn.' They start to dance and hook arms, singing at the top of their voices. 'Too ra loo ra too ra loo rye aye…'

Ruby slides in beside me at the door. 'He's so good.'

'Yeah. He really is.'

'He's hot, too. And I don't even like gingers.'

I suddenly become defensive. 'His hair isn't ginger, it's auburn.'

'Nope, that's definitely ginger,' she says, twirling her pen in her fingers. 'Not like carrot-top orange, more a dark ginger…'

I nudge her in the arm. 'That's enough, you, focus on your assignment, please. Christy is a cultural history guru; you'd do well to take some notes.'

'I wonder if he's single,' Ruby says.

Danny calls out to me. 'Come on, Eve-lyn!'

Ruby's hands fly to her face. 'Oh my God, he so likes you!'

I shake my head and give her a bemused look.

'He knows your name.'

'That's not a big deal.' I shrug, because it isn't a big deal. Honestly, no big deal.

'Yeah, well if it's no big deal, why are your cheeks bright red?'

Danny strums down the last chord, and the crowd high-five and whoop around him, emptying their wallets and pockets into his cap on the ground. He waves and smiles across at me.

Damn it. I don't know if it's his smile or his voice or his eyes or the way he looks at me and seems to change the landscape, the light, my mood… My stomach flips.

I need to keep myself in check with this guy. Especially if he keeps surprising me this way, because I am a complete sucker for surprises, and brown eyes with a mischievous little twinkle…

CHAPTER FOURTEEN

The moment I arrive for my shift and push through the double doors, I can tell something is wrong. Christy is early; he's got an opened bottle by him and it looks as though he's on his second whiskey already, sitting grave and sunken at the counter. Colm is behind the bar, leaning against the cash register, his brow furrowed with worry.

'Everything okay?' I ask as I hang up my coat and tie my apron around my waist.

Colm gestures at a stool. 'You'd better take a seat a second, Evelyn. I've had some bad news – a meeting with the bank manager.'

Christy slams his glass down on the counter, muttering obscenities.

I shake my head. 'I'm sorry, Colm, you've lost me.'

He steps forward and places both hands on the counter to support his weight. There's a veil of sweat on his forehead, more than I've ever seen before; things must be bad.

'Over the years, I've borrowed a lot of money, remortgaged several times against an outstanding loan, and I'm not able to make the repayments. Now the bank has caught up with me. The long and short of it is this place is haemorrhaging money. I've not turned a decent profit in donkey's years. I have three months to clear the loan or they take the pub. So I've no option but to sell up.'

Christy splutters into his hand, padding along his waistcoat for a handkerchief. 'There must be a way to get more people in.

Look at the difference Evelyn has made already. The custom is still there. Have an open-mic night, a quiz, start doing some hot meals… You can do it, Colm.'

Colm raises his bandaged hand in the air and shakes his head.

'No, I can't. Physically, I'm not able. Hand on heart, I'm exhausted and ready to give it up. I've done it the one way all my life and I've not got the fire to learn a new way. Young people these days want so much, all these trendy bars in town. There's no way I can compete with that craic. Rosie Munroe's time is up – sometimes you've just got to admit defeat and call it a day.'

No. I can hardly process what I'm hearing. I slump on to a bar stool and try to steady my thoughts. This can't be happening; we've just got under way. No way am I ready to call it a day. I want this job. I *need* this job! If this place closes, I'll have to go back to that creepy teacher-recruitment guy. And even then there's no guarantee of a post because he's never called me back. Not one of the recruitment agencies has. Worse still, without a job, I'll have to go home to Ballybeg, back to living with my mother and even back to Mrs O'Driscoll with a tyrannosaurus-sized tail between my legs.

I run my hands through my hair, trying to think of what this actually means for me.

No more pub, no more Dublin, no more independence or adventure or possibility or hope. I hear the strum of the guitar start up outside. And no more Danny. I put my head in my hands. Maybe in time that could have led to something, but now I'll never know; everything that was just starting to emerge has been cut short, unplugged, shut down… I can't help feel like something special was brewing, and this makes this blow even harder to accept. Even if I stay in Dublin, get a job in another pub, it's not going to be anything like here.

I run my hand over the counter, here where history was made. Where Rosie's vision for a better future took root.

'You can't just give up like this, Colm,' I beseech him. 'We've got to fight This place can't just close. There's too much history here. You say you can't compete with the trendy bars, but you don't need to; you are in a totally different league. They are all the same, copy-cat kits rolled out onto every high street in every major city in the world. We've been really busy the last few weeks; every single day we get more and more customers through the door. Word is spreading! There is nowhere like this place, drenched with character and tradition and an atmosphere that you simply can't create in a soulless franchise. There is no other pub like this in the whole world, and there never will be. That's what makes it special. Makes it worth fighting for.'

Christy looks up. 'She's right, you know.'

He stands up from his stool and struts into the centre of the floor, swinging his handkerchief over towards the top corner table.

'Oscar Wilde wrote volumes in that corner, always sat beside the fire. Too tight to pay for his own heating, they say. But I think he was earwigging, on the lookout for material.' He pivots on his heel back towards us, pointing beyond the bar. 'And out back there, in the old dance hall, that's where the rebels and the revolutionaries gathered – Wolfe Tone, Daniel O'Connell. That's where they had their secret meetings. They knew no one worth their salt would ever give them up. If they did, they'd have nowhere to drink.'

He raises his chin to the mounted vinyl on the walls, his eyes glinting at a signed Thin Lizzy sleeve. 'Many a famous musician climbed up to the roof garden after hours and spent the night under the stars with their favourite landlady. Rosie was very… *hospitable*, shall we say. The hostess with the mostess. And didn't she know how to run a cracking bar; for a magical time this place, these walls, these seats, this space held the heart and soul of this city.'

Colm is nodding, the mist of nostalgia in his eyes. 'It's true. Hard to imagine now, but it was like that once. Back in the day, people didn't sit in their homes; they went out and socialised every night of the week. Way back when the English landed, they used to wonder why the Irish were happy despite the poverty, and it was because we had this rich sociability in our lives. A sense of connectedness. Coming together in a welcoming space gave us the chance to really know each other, to tell our stories. In many ways, the pub is the cornerstone of our culture. A culture of the spirit, the music and the imagination.'

'And the best Guinness in town,' I chime in. Colm smiles at me with sadness in his eyes.

Christy helps himself to another slug of whiskey, then walks with it to the fireplace, taking a seat in the chair he ascribed to Oscar Wilde. 'We can't just hand hundreds of years over to a greasy-fingered banker. You need to fight harder than that, Colm. What would Rosie Munroe do if she was here?'

Colm wipes a bandaged hand down his face. 'She'd have shot him with both barrels.'

'Exactly. And she'd be right. And what are you doing? Only rolling over like a docile dog.'

Colm raises his voice a notch. 'Times are different now, Christy; no one can fight the system and win. I'm done. I've not got the fight in me. If I could save this place, believe me I would. I have memories in every crack and crevice of it. I've got three months to pay back the loan with interest or I'll have to sell up,' he explains. 'Right now, it's costing me every day I stay open.'

I lean against the counter and try to take in everything he's saying. I can see that he's losing money because the interest on his loan is so high. But we've quadrupled the footfall here in a matter of a few weeks, and every day that's getting stronger. Once we get people over the threshold, they love the place. True, we are nowhere near as busy as the other pubs and bars in town, but that's because we haven't even touched the surface in terms of passing trade and tourists. We could definitely make that happen: just some good advertising, live music and gigs, some social media… completely fixable.

'I could help you, Colm,' I tell him. 'I can work longer shifts, try out some ideas, drum up some business. Redecorate the interior.' I look round me. The tables are old, marked and chipped from years of use. The painted walls are stained yellow with smoke and there's a red flock velvet border that's curling up in more places than it's stuck to the wall.

Colm scratches his neck and looks around as if he's studying the place for the first time, scrutinising it. 'That's part of its charm, though. We're not a high-street chain or some kind of theme bar; this is a traditional Irish pub, warts and all.'

'She's not saying to change it completely, Colm, she's suggesting a bit of a freshen-up, that's all. A lick of paint, that kind of thing.' Christy winks over at me while Colm processes the idea.

'I can't afford it,' Colm says. 'Painters, decorators, materials, equipment. It all adds up, and cash is tight.'

Before I even think it through, the words are out of my mouth. 'I'll do it for you. I'll get whatever I can at the market and keep your costs as low as possible. I think it could look absolutely amazing, and who knows, we could have this place packed to the rafters again!'

Colm strokes his chin and doesn't look convinced.

'We haven't even got enough punters to balance the books. I think the days of people queuing for a pint at Rosie Munroe's are well and truly finished.'

'Don't say that. We're already getting more people through the doors. And you're paying me to be here anyway, so I may as well multitask. After all, it's my job on the line if this place gets any quieter.'

Colm still isn't convinced. 'It's very nice of you, Evelyn, but I need to let go of this place. I'm tired. Burnt out, as they say. I need some rest, so maybe in a way it's a blessing in disguise.'

I understand. I can see it in his body: he's worn out.

Christy walks over to the mantelpiece cluttered up with old antiques – clocks and horses and brass figurines along with sepia prints of suited men and wavy-haired women sitting in a row at the bar counter, their eyes laughing as they raise a toast to the camera. He studies the collection and pulls out a framed shot from the back, wiping the dust from the glass pane with his sleeve.

'Here it is.' He walks back over to us holding the frame in front of him. 'Rosie Munroe's at its peak.'

I study the picture. It's hard to believe this is the same place. The exterior is whitewashed, with an old-style hand-painted sign in red and black. There are seats outside, with plenty of people sitting at them – men and women side by side. Steel kegs are stacked up by the open double doors, always a sure sign of a successful business. In the middle of the doorway is a tall, strong-looking woman standing with her hands on her hips, a wide, welcoming smile on her face – Rosie Munroe.

'It's too late,' says Colm. 'I'm going to have to sell. I can't run it any more and I don't know anyone who will take it on, even just on a lease. Believe me, if I did, I'd sign it over in a heartbeat.'

Somebody to take it on? I thought his only option was to pay the loan off or sell the pub. But lease it?

'What do you mean exactly, Colm?' I ask.

'If I thought there was somebody experienced out there who could turn the place around and generate enough profit to get us out of this mess, they could have it. I could draw up a lease agreement this minute. But that's never going to happen – who's mad enough to take on a failing business? So I'm going to cut my losses, shut the door for good and just hand it over to the bank now. At least that way I'll spare myself the stress.'

My mind leaps forward to possibilities. I still have some savings – maybe even enough to pay a lease. Could I do this? Is it what I've been waiting for? There are a thousand reasons to hold my tongue and just back away. I can hear my mother's voice in my ear – *daft idea... inexperienced... money pit... pubs closing their doors every day of the week... long hours... zero holidays...* But just as I told Ruby, if I make this choice and it turns out to be a mistake, however it goes, I'll learn from it. And I'll know I did it for my own reasons.

I want to stay here, of that I am certain. I want to save Rosie Munroe's and maybe, just maybe, I could make a go of it. Put my own stamp on it. Develop the ideas needed to restore it to its former glory. I know I've not got any real experience, but who does? No landlady I ever heard of went to publican university. Rosie Munroe certainly didn't, and look at all she achieved! I arrived here in Dublin without a clue as to how my life was going to go, and so far, it's working out better than I ever hoped. I'm happier here and now than I have been in years. So why not? Even if I end up failing... well at least I will have tried, I gave it a go, I'll have no regrets. After all, it should be a hell of a lot easier walking away from *this* if it fails than it was walking away from my marriage. And I survived that.

I need to ask myself something: what is it I want to do? *Really* want to do? I could take the first teaching job the recruitment agent offers me, a respectable post that pays the bills. But if there is something I have learnt so far, it's that the safe option isn't always the right option. I did that before, I did it with St Mary's and I did it with my marriage; I did it for my parents and I did it for James, and in the end, I couldn't keep it up. I couldn't paint the happy smile on my face and pretend that I was fulfilled and committed. And that's what's brought me here, to the riskiest choices in my life. Splitting with James, jacking in my job and serving behind this bar feels right, feels like a fit.

I came to Dublin to figure out what I wanted, and I've found it. And now that it's under threat, am I just going to let it go? Let it slip away?

I know the answer to that.

Rosie didn't just shrug her shoulders and give up when faced with a challenge. She didn't take no for an answer. And it really takes that kind of heart-racing courage and fighting spirit to achieve anything. If she couldn't find a way, she *made* a way.

I've done safe, I've done easy, I've tried to live small. Now I'm ready to go hard or go home.

Fighting for Rosie Munroe's is kind of like fighting for myself, for the space to pursue something meaningful, to take a risk and believe that with vision and hard work and the right people around me, I can make it happen.

There's only one answer to this.

CHAPTER FIFTEEN

'Me,' I say aloud.

'Pardon?' Both men shoot me a look.

'I'll take on the lease. I'll take on Rosie Munroe's.'

Colm sighs a sympathetic smile and clasps his hands together. 'That's awful nice of you, Evelyn, but I don't want you saddled with a redundant business. This isn't like teaching. This is hard graft twenty-four seven. At its best it's full of drunkards and at its worst it's dead, quiet as a mausoleum, and that's when the hours are long and lonely and the overheads suffocate you. I appreciate your offer, but I couldn't do that to you. I couldn't let you do it to yourself.'

I take a deep breath. My entire body is battling itself. The left side of my brain is telling me this is not a sound investment. The right side wants more – to tear down the cobwebs and throw open the doors and fill the place with light and music and laughter… And what about those extra rooms? A dance hall? A roof garden? My stomach has folded in on itself at the enormity of the decision and the prospect of failure, but my heart is bursting with the possibility – no, the *certainty* that it won't be anything less than a roaring success.

I look around the bar at the clusters of tables, at the time-worn stone walls and the great big turf fireplace, the old high stools and the polished hardwood floor that has been walked across by the good and the great for the last half-century. The real-life theatre of human life in all its rawness: sadness and celebration, passions and friendships, songs and music.

I have an idea. I raise my finger to them. 'Don't do anything until I get back.' Then I rush out through the double doors into the street.

I don't even wait for Danny to finish his song. I run to his side and curl my hand around his ear, explaining my chance – *our* chance. Then I step back and watch his face as he processes what I just told him.

'And you think I could help?' he asks, a half-smile playing on his lips.

'Yes,' I nod. 'You know the area, you know the city. You know about musicians and where to find them and how to book them and what they need to set up. And I think that's really what Rosie's USP is all about.'

'USP?'

'Unique selling point. Rosie's was a famous music venue; if we can bring that back to life, then we're on our way.'

Danny stands, squinting up at the old building. 'Have you ever done anything like this before?'

I shake my head. 'That's why I figure I should do it now.'

'You are a bit crazy, you know. Or are you all like this down the country?'

'Not as crazy as you are, standing out here on the street day after day with that amazing voice of yours. We could do it; between us we have everything we need.'

'Us?' He rubs his face with his hands.

'You and me, together as a team. If we don't do it, the pub will shut forever. Simple as that. And if we shy away from this, we're probably going to shy away from everything. This is one of those chances to feel the fear but do it anyway. All the financial risk is mine, but I know I need you to make it work. I think we'd be a great team, Danny.'

He looks at me, that same half-smile still on his face. 'Really? How could you know that?'

'Right, I'll tell you how. I hear you singing your heart out on the street every day, come rain or shine, so I know that you are really hard-working. You read people really well. Remember those little schoolchildren reaching for the stars? You can change their mood, lift their spirits in an instant. You never sing a note out of tune or without giving every performance your absolute all, so I know that getting things right is important to you. You ran straight in to help me when the brawl broke out, so I know you're kind and chivalrous, and I know that you already know your way around the bar because you've helped Colm when he's been stuck. And if I get another fat lip, I know who I'd like to fix me up.' I point to my top lip. 'See how well it healed? That's down to you.'

Danny hooks his hand around the back of his neck and throws his head back. 'You completely believe in this, don't you?'

'Yes. Completely.'

'What do you have in mind?'

'A complete refurb of the pub and the stage area at the back. Then a grand opening where you book us the best up-and-coming band in Dublin and we pack out the house. After that, the sky is the limit.'

'We'll have to do a research date. Get some inspiration, see what's already out there, check out the competition.'

'Yes!' I want to jump up and down on the spot. I knew I could convince him. 'You're on. Anywhere, any time. So you're with me?' I ask him.

'Let's do it. Proposal accepted.' And we shake on the deal.

Then I wrap my arms around his neck and whisper, 'Thank you, you won't regret this, I promise.'

*

At the end of my shift, Colm signs the lease over to me and I scribble my name on the dotted line.

'You're now officially the new licensee of Rosie Munroe's and the first female landlady since the great woman herself. I wish you every success, Evelyn.' And he hands me the keys.

This is getting real.

CHAPTER SIXTEEN

Danny's picking me up outside my house at eight so we can check out some other music venues and see what we are up against in terms of competition. The ink isn't even dry on the contract and yet I'm getting ready to go on a market research date.

Which gives me all of twenty minutes to get ready.

I pull out my suitcase to find something suitable to wear – I just wear jeans and a T-shirt to the pub, so that won't do. I didn't bring much with me to Dublin, and looking at the small folded pile that is now my entire wardrobe, I realise James may have had a point – pretty much everything I own looks like it belongs on a Conservative politician at least twenty years my senior... who is in mourning. The only thing I have that's not black is a slinky, silky cobalt-blue dress Tara gave me for my birthday last year. I guess I kind of brought it as a personal dare, a challenge to myself, like keeping clothes three sizes too small in your wardrobe with a half-baked intention of fitting into them again one day.

I need to get a move on, no overthinking. But isn't this dress a bit tight? A bit short? These heels a bit high?

I hold it up. Actually, I think it might be just the thing.

I blow-dry my hair so it's got a bit of shine and movement. Next: make-up. I've been watching Ruby apply hers, and that winged flick she does with her kohl eyeliner is incredible, so I give the smoky look a go, just enough to accent the colour of my eyes. Then a dusting of blush and a slick of lipstick. Okay, I think that should do it.

I tug at my dress; there's no time to change now. I wriggle in it until it hangs just right, then turn to the full-length mirror on the back of the door. I watch the look of fear dissolve from my face and a smile relax across my lips. *Wow.* I smile at what I see, because it's been far too long since I last looked like this. I'm not saying I'm gorgeous by any means, but I do look decent. I look like someone happy and hopeful and confident, and like I may just belong in this city after all.

For a moment it is as if I'm looking at a different person, or someone familiar but changed… I'm seeing myself through different eyes. I practise saying my name, as if I'm trying on a new identity. I thrust out my hand to shake that of an imaginary stranger. *Yes, I am Evelyn Dooley. That's right, I'm the landlady of Rosie Munroe's. Yes, I am bouncing from one day to the next. But yes, I am pretty proud of myself actually, thank you for asking.*

I imagine it's Danny in front of me. I try to picture what he sees, what he thinks. How long has it been since someone found me attractive?

Tara slips her head around the door. She opens her mouth, but no words come out. I smooth my dress down, in an effort to make it longer. 'Sorry, it's too much. I should change.'

'Are you crazy? You look *incredible*. But where are you going to at this time?'

'Oh Tara, I've got so much to tell you. Today has been crazy. But I need to run now. I've got a date.'

Tara's eyes widen. 'A *date*? Evelyn Dooley, you sly thing! Tell me everything in the morning.'

I hear someone climbing the steps outside the house, and before he even has a chance to ring the bell, I've opened the door and am standing right in front of him, my bag over my shoulder, ready to go.

A date! A proper date with an actual live, incredibly attractive man, face to face, at night, in real time. No big group to fall back on, no mutual friends to defuse the pressure, no safety net. Just him and me and a vision to make this dream a reality.

Am I crazy?

Probably.

But I'm too excited to care.

We walk the yellow-lit streets, through a dark archway and along a stone-walled alley where, under a lone flickering blue sign we knock on the side door of what looks like a shut-down warehouse. Within seconds, a long-haired guy in a leather waistcoat greets Danny with affection and leads us down a tight stairwell, the walls covered in graffiti and droplets of condensation.

The door to the basement opens and I'm overwhelmed by the scene. It's dark and dingy but jammed with a completely different crowd to that of Rosie Munroe's. This place has a real mix of beautiful, energetic people dancing and clapping and beating out the drumbeat with their fingers and their feet. They are a wild, raw, rhythmic tribe with piercings and tattoos and asymmetric hair and an air of effortless, bohemian, nihilistic chic. I relax. This is the kind of place you can just blend in; people don't come to catwalk or people-watch – you can be yourself here. Besides, the music is so good, everyone is beyond caring about anything else. I pull my hair down and shake it out; I can feel the vibrations of the bass in the soles of my feet.

The bar is like an old Western saloon bar. I love the look of the brandy-coloured lighting, the dark wood and leather booths, the candles burning in old wax-covered bottles – heaven. Danny looks over his shoulder to ensure I'm all right, his fingers finding his way to mine and threading through. 'So you don't get lost.' He winks.

We take two stools at the low counter curving along the side of the room. All the bar staff seem to know Danny; they clap him on the back and smile their hellos.

'What do you think?'

I nod. 'I like it. It's certainly busy. Do you think we could do something like this on our side of the river?'

He widens his eyes. 'Definitely. There's a queue snaking around the corner here all evening, and if you don't get in before ten, you've got no chance. So plenty of potential. Good news for us, eh? I think a decent music venue is what people are crying out for. You get tired of seeing the same old scene played out again and again. Nothing like a live gig, best feeling in the world.' We clink bottles and our heads turn to the acoustic set on stage.

The longer I spend with Danny, the more time I want to spend with him. This place is exactly what I had I mind for Rosie's. I knew I could count on him. He gets it, he gets me, and he gets what I want for the pub.

He leans into my ear so I can hear him. 'The best new bands cut their teeth here. Often record company guys come to hear the latest sounds, gauge the reception of the crowd – scout the next big thing. Of course, most people just come here to listen.' We turn our attention back to the stage and watch a new band perform their set.

'What do you think?' Danny asks me when they've finished their first song.

I blow out my cheeks. 'Phenomenal stage presence. They've got something there, but the lead singer is in the wrong key. He's in D, it's too low for him. I think he needs more bass; a saxophone would also lift the middle. The drums need to pull back. A little too much going on in parts, but what a unique sound. I loved it.'

Danny blinks at me, and an incredulous smile spreads across his face.

'Are you serious? Did you just make all that stuff up?'

I shake my head. 'Of course not. I studied music at uni, I picked a few things up.'

'I think you're spot on. Agree completely. They're called Supanova. I'll pass on all your hot tips.'

'You know them?'

'Absolutely. That's why we're here. If you like them, we could ask if they're up for doing the grand opening of Rosie's.'

My heart twists in my chest and for a second I imagine what it would be like, what it could be like, to have all these people, this sound, this energy under our roof. Yes. Yes, yes, yes.

He smiles at me. 'Looks like our market research date is going to pay off.'

'Do you ever play here?'

'Used to.'

I can tell by the way he slowly lifts his bottle to his lips that it's not something he wants to get into. He taps his fingers on the bar then looks back at the stage. I close my eyes and listen to the music, breathing in my surroundings, soaking up the bustle and movement of the people – all these glorious strangers swirling around me.

'Thanks,' he says, when there's a pause.

'For what?'

'Not being pushy.' He locks eyes with me for a moment.

I smile. I know exactly what he means. I've always found questions difficult, small talk even worse; most people don't seem to notice when they cross the boundaries of what you want to talk about. At parties, I'd often excuse myself and sneak off to stand outside the back door, or sit on the stairs – anywhere quiet and out of the way – for a breather. Some time out. Often there'd be other people there too, just like me, needing space. And we'd nod at each other and then avert our eyes, busy ourselves inspecting the ceiling or our fingernails with understanding and respectful silence. This was our perfect pause, a sliver of sanctuary, our wordless place.

When the song ends, we get to our feet, clapping and whistling for more.

'I just love this place,' Danny calls to me over the crowd. 'I've been coming here for years.'

'So did you grow up in Dublin?' I ask him when the noise has died down again.

He nods.

'Which part?'

'All over really, both sides of the river. Me and my twin brother were brought up in care, so from the age of five onwards we got moved around a bit, different foster families, different schools, different care homes, that kind of thing.'

I don't know what to say, how to react. This couldn't be more different from my own upbringing, with a family tree I can trace back hundreds of years within a square mile. Danny looks back up to the band, sensing my self-consciousness.

'I'm hoping that you had some good experiences, but I guess that isn't always the case,' I say, circling the rim of my glass with my finger, hoping I'm not asking too much.

'It was all right. My mother was into drugs in a big way, so a neighbour tipped off the police. One day we came in from school and the door had been knocked down. We were swept up out of there and that was the end of that. I don't remember too much of those early days. But the social workers tried their best for us; they promised they wouldn't split Rory and me up, and they kept their word on that. So wherever Rory went, I was close behind.'

'What was it like?'

I get the sense that he wants to tell me. That now that we're here, in this great new project together, it's important that I understand and get a sense of who he is beneath the talented musician on the corner.

'It was okay. Some families were great, made you feel like they wanted you there but they couldn't keep you for various reasons; others were the complete opposite. So I guess you end up putting the bad ones down to experience and hoping the next one will be better, that it might even turn out to be your forever home with your forever family.'

My heart swells in my chest for the two little boys holding out hope as they were moved from place to place. I know exactly what it's like to dream about a forever family, to pin your hopes on something and believe that once it comes along, everything else will fall into place.

'Did that ever happen?' I ask him. 'Please say it did.'

He shakes his head, but smiles. 'I'm still waiting. I haven't given up on that particular dream just yet.'

'Well, we've got that in common,' I tell him. 'I was married. I thought I'd have a forever family by now.'

He raises his eyebrows. 'And what happened with that?'

'He didn't want it as much as I did. So it was a deal-breaker in the end. We're divorced now.'

'A break-up with paperwork. Ouch.' He nods slowly, like we're starting to make sense to each other. 'Is that why you came to Dublin? To start all over again?'

'That was the idea.' And sitting here with this beautiful man, checking out bands for our brand-new venture, I'd say it was probably the best idea I've had in a long, long time.

Long after the band has finished playing, Danny and I are still deep in conversation.

'Do you ever write your own music?' I ask.

He takes a deep breath before he answers. 'We used to.'

That reticence again. *We* used to. Is Danny fresh from a big break-up too? I know better than to push. He'll tell me if he wants me to know. I take a sip of my drink, give him some space to choose his words.

'Rory and I used to play together. We used to play here. It was right up there that we were picked up by a record company.' He nods towards the stage.

'Congratulations! To be honest, I'm not surprised. Your voice is incredible.'

He blushes and waves his hand. 'Thanks, but Rory was actually the singer. And the songwriter. I was just guitarist and general slave.'

I am desperate to know why he plays on the street if he had a record deal. What happened? Were they dropped? Did they turn the deal down? And where is Rory? I've never seen anyone else playing with Danny on the corner – did the record label take Rory and leave his brother? Again, I wait; if he wants to tell me, I'm sure he will. And if not, that's his decision, not mine.

He presses his hands together like a steeple in front of his lips.

'But Rory went and died. So that was that. Rory died and took our world with him.'

I reach out for his hand. 'Oh Danny, I'm so sorry.'

'Me too.' He raises his glass and I do the same. 'To starting over.' He toasts.

I nod and throw down my drink in one. And here, half drunk, in the early hours of the morning, with one hand curled around my glass and the other round the fingers of a beautiful, kind and gifted man, I feel overwhelmed, emotional at the way we have found each other. There are so many people in this city, in this world, and somehow I'm sitting across from this one. Somehow, amid this heaving crowd, we've managed to catch each other's eye. And it feels perfectly right.

He sweeps his thumb over mine. 'Ready to go?' he asks. 'Another big day tomorrow.'

I nod, and he squeezes my hand and holds it tightly as we push our way against the throng, out into the new dawn light together.

CHAPTER SEVENTEEN

The band is booked. Danny pulled in a favour and Supanova have agreed to play here on our opening night, which is just incredible. The moment word got out, we had people phoning us up wanting to know whether it was true, and we were able to confirm that yes, it's actually happening. Ruby has agreed to take over our social media campaign, so already the details have been shared all over the country and beyond. She's a whizz with tech and graphics; already she's mustered up a couple of hundred followers and created a buzz about our launch, posting old footage she's found online of bands playing to packed-out crowds, sharing the story of Rosie Munroe and her infamous pub crawl for equality. Yesterday she told me that she even went to an after-school club voluntarily to ask for help building our webpage.

Danny and I have decided that the only way we are going to get the place really up to scratch is to close the pub for five whole days, Monday to Friday, and have our grand opening on Saturday night. That'll give us a (very tightly scheduled) chance to refurbish the disused rooms, clean everything out, set it up as we want it and drum up some excitement on local radio and in the newspapers, getting word out that Rosie Munroe's is under new management and ready to take over the city.

Tomorrow, our contractors arrive. I've had to dip into my savings for all of this. We could do it ourselves, but it wouldn't be up to standard and it would take a lot longer than five days. So I've bitten the bullet and pulled out all the stops. First impressions count, and I can't afford to get this wrong. If Rosie's exceeds everyone's expectations on the first night, then word will spread, our reputation will precede us and I'll make the money back to cover it. That's my business plan, basic and built on common sense. Danny has sourced the builders, the electricians, the painters and the plumbers. He's got us mates' rates, so I'm hoping we're going to come in on budget and be completely ready and looking sensational in time for Saturday night, with no last-minute emergencies. Our grand reopening. Which will be exciting. And terrifying.

Danny and I spend the whole of Sunday cleaning out the back rooms that have been shut off and haven't seen the light of day for over a decade. We fill a skip with black bin bags of crap just from downstairs. It takes us eight hours straight. Once that's done, we knock down the thin partition blocking off the old dance hall that Christy mentioned out the back. Just for a little peek, to see if it actually exists or if it was just a figment of his whiskey-fuelled nostalgia. Danny kicks the painted chipboard down with little effort and we step through eagerly.

Wow, it exists all right. Christy wasn't making it up. It's the size of a tennis court. Chandeliers, embossed wallpaper, marble pillars... it blows my mind.

'Speakers,' Danny says suddenly, snapping me out of my reverie. 'Stick it on your checklist. We'll need top-quality sound to fill this space.'

I gasp, holding my hand to my chest.

'What's up?' he asks, concern in his eyes.

'It's all suddenly getting very real.' I meet his gaze. 'I was just picturing what it's going to be like when it's finished. I still can't quite believe we're doing this. This room! It's perfect, it couldn't be more perfect.'

Danny takes to the centre of the floor and motions for me to join him in a waltz. I step into his open arms and position his hands, one on my waist and one raised in front.

'You don't know what you're doing, do you?' I say, as he treads on my toes for the third time.

He shuffles backwards and forwards and shakes his head. 'No clue.'

So I take his hand in mine and slide my arm along his shoulder. 'Follow my lead,' I tell him, and we step out. 'One two three, one two three, one two three… turn.'

We sashay and swing around the floor a few more times, Danny picking the steps up very quickly and trying to add his own lifts and improvisations.

'I bet your parents danced like this,' he says as we slow down.

'They did. My father used to take my mum up to Dublin for weekends when they were first married. They'd go on the train, spend the day at the race track and then go out for dinner and dancing.' I remember photos of my mother in a party dress dipping backwards in my father's arms. He used to say he thought there was a lovely charm in meeting somebody this way: inviting them to dance, swaying to the music together, exchanging smiles while the music played – no swiping to the left for these guys.

'You're quite the romantic,' I tease Danny. 'Serenades, waltzes, offers to walk country girls home.'

'Can't help myself,' he says, and steps closer to me. From the way he hesitates, I get the impression he's unsure if it's okay to come any closer. He's unsure whether I *want* him any closer.

But I do. In this moment, I absolutely do.

He's staring at me, contemplating his next move. I want him to just go for it. I bite down on my lower lip and close my eyes. I'm not yet ready to make the first move, but I won't resist him if he does. I can smell his scent; I can feel the warmth of his chest against mine. We stand motionless, two dancers stuck in a pose, neither sure how to act around the other.

'So how about you, do you consider yourself a closet romantic?'

I shake my head. 'No, I don't think so. Well, maybe. I'm not sure. Once upon a time, perhaps.' A memory comes flashing into my mind. 'When I was sixteen, I was asked to go to the graduation ball by a boy in my class. I was so surprised, so taken aback – for lots of different reasons: I'd never been asked out before, I didn't realise that he'd even noticed me and I'd kind of resigned myself to not going at all.'

'Why not?'

'Because it wasn't me somehow. I'd never done anything so public, so exposed like that before, and I never did anything like it afterwards. It's almost like it happened to someone else. You'd have to know me to understand. I was the kind of girl who wouldn't go out on a Friday night in case I fell behind in my school work.'

He laughed. 'I doubt that.'

'It's true. I didn't.'

'So what happened?'

'My mother made me a beautiful dress, my sister did my hair, we took loads of photos before even leaving the house. But when I arrived at the dance hall, a beautiful big gilded room like this, he was with someone else. He had another partner. He'd changed his mind and never bothered telling me.'

'The bastard,' Danny says. 'Tell me where he lives, the little shit.' He tightens his arm around my waist. 'What did you do? I hope you went and smacked him.'

I laugh at the thought. 'I just slipped out the side door. I went to the cinema instead. Sat in the darkened seats all by myself with a big box of popcorn until it was time to go home. And when I got in, my mother and sister were waiting up, excited to hear all about the evening.'

'What did you tell them?'

'I pretended that everything had gone wonderfully, that my date was a perfect gent and that I'd had the best night of my life. They went to bed smiling. And that was a fair enough result for me.'

'Do you mind if I tell you something?' he asks. 'I mean, I don't want you to take it the wrong way.'

'I won't.'

He pauses, choosing his words carefully, I suspect. I'm shitting myself. I have no idea what he's going to tell me and I promised I'd take it. My stomach drops in dread.

'Well… it's just when you talk about yourself, it's almost like you're talking about someone else. I know you went to university, but not many people study for so long just to then quit their respectable job and work in a pub. You say you're quiet and shy, but then I see you peel two angry teenagers apart. You say you keep to yourself, but you've totally taken Ruby under your wing, giving her your time and your support to help her make something of her life. I guess I'm just trying to figure you out, Evelyn Dooley.'

I hesitate. I don't have to explain myself, not to him, not to anyone, but as we sway back and forth in the middle of this silent dance floor, I suddenly realise that I want him to know me – really know me, with all my seeming contradictions. I genuinely care what he thinks, *how* he thinks. I want to explore him, get inside his head as much as he seems to want to get inside mine. And the only way for that to happen is to be honest, to be open, to tell the truth without shame or apology.

'You're right,' I begin. 'Because I think I am talking about two people. I used to be Evelyn O'Connor, the conscientious wife and teacher, the dutiful daughter. The one who worked all the time. Who went along with what others decided, even what they thought was best for me. But these days, I don't feel like I'm any of those things any more. Right now, I'm trying to figure out who I really am, and to be honest, I'm beginning to wonder if I'll ever find the answer.'

Danny searches my eyes, a half-smile playing on his lips.

'Everyone feels that way sometimes, but not too many people take action. Not too many people have the guts to change things for the better.'

'You think? I've always kind of thought of that as weakness, a failure, like I quit. But the way you say it makes it feel like it was something else, something brave.'

We continue to sway on in silence before he looks at me again. 'Good.'

'Good what?'

'You're starting to see yourself like I see you. And that's good.'

He steps back, bows and offers his hand.

'Evelyn Dooley, may I please have this dance?'

'The pleasure is all mine.' I laugh and we press our bodies closer, dancing slowly on this dusty floor to some sort of soundless music that it seems only we can hear. I tilt my face towards his neck, and he pulls me up by my waist onto my tiptoes. His lips brush against my cheek, and this, the lightest of touches, sends a current through my skin, a shock that makes my entire body shudder.

He whispers by my ear, his breath warm and close. 'If you want me to stop, tell me now.' I say nothing. I can't speak; there is no air in my lungs. And I don't want him to stop. Slowly he brushes his lips upwards along my face, kissing me where my hairline meets my temple.

'Or now,' he says again, his voice deep and low.

Still I say nothing. I want more. His lips travel down, now against the hollow of my cheekbone. His mouth is ready, warm and waiting like a question, with lips half parted, his breath suspended.

'Or…'

'Now,' I gasp as I reach up and pull him to me, breathless in a new and urgent way.

Our lips meet, the current now coursing through me from my mouth right down to my tiptoed feet. Danny groans softly, low in his throat, and then his arms circle around me, hoisting me closer to him. The space around us evaporates. I can hear nothing but his breath, I feel nothing but his body. There is only now, and us, and this energy we have between us, and in this moment I feel infinite.

His hands are everywhere, up my back and over my arms, and suddenly he's kissing me harder, deeper, with a fervent, urgent need I've never known before. There is no time, and yet we have all the time. He is like a new universe, uncharted sky; I want to explore every inch of him. I want to go in so far, so deep; I want to get lost in him.

I've had a glimpse, a taste, and I realise I'll never have enough. Something in me has opened up, unlocked, exploded. This is like the Big Bang, the explosive pinpoint in time when all events come together in a storm of potent energy, in exactly the right way to make everything else possible.

Trembling, I knot my fists in his shirt, pulling him towards me harder, because I felt it. Just now.

Because Danny Foy is my Big Bang.

CHAPTER EIGHTEEN

As I walk up the stairs, ready to collapse into bed after a full day of cleaning in the pub, I check my twelve-page checklist one more time. There's so much going on tomorrow that I've had to write down a timeline of tasks, everything in five-minute chunks so we know who is where, what they are doing and how much they cost. We absolutely cannot afford to balls it up. Not only is the lease eating through my savings, but so is all the work that needs doing to bring it up to scratch: materials and labour and then new stock seeing as Colm really only sold Guinness and whiskey to his regulars. Then there's been a budget overspill into things that never crossed my mind, like glassware, staff uniforms, mousetraps and stacks of new toilet paper that's not yellowed around the edges.

No sooner do I shut the front door of our flat behind me than there's a knock. And a tiny voice calling my name. 'Helloo, Evelyn? Are you there? Can I have a word?'

It's Moira. The last person in the world I'm in the mood to have a conversation with now, but what choice do I have? She knows I'm in, I can hardly say no. And it's her house. She has the power to throw me out on the front step if she takes a notion. And from the way she treats her granddaughter, I wouldn't put that past her…

I paste on my best fake smile. Tara does it for a living, so I guess I can do it for five minutes to appease my landlady. I open the door, but just a smidge.

'Hi, Moira, lovely to see you. What can I do for you?'

'It's about Ruby.' I open the door fully. 'We have an appointment tomorrow to meet with her headmaster. I was thinking, seeing as you've been such a help to her, that maybe you could go on my behalf. Talk to them about her, you know, give them hell. She's been doing a lot better since you've been helping her; she likes calling in to the pub and doing her homework down there. It's what I've said all along – she just needed the right help.'

'Tomorrow? Oh Moira, any other time, I would love to go. But I've taken on Rosie Munroe's and we're working our socks off all week to get it ready for Saturday – our grand opening.'

Moira widens her eyes and coughs into her fist. 'That wasn't the answer I was hoping for, Evelyn.'

'Let Ruby know I'm really sorry, and I hope it goes well. Fill me in when you get back.' I step back to close the door; I need my bed now, and my eyes are stinging with tiredness.

Moira juts her chin in the air. 'I told her as much.'

'What do you mean?'

'I told her not to expect anything from you. That you'd be busy and make your excuses. People don't just drop everything for others – it doesn't work like that.' She is staring at me, arms folded, like I owe her more.

I take a deep breath, ready to reiterate my reasons for not going. It's not because I can't be bothered; it's because I can't abandon the refurbishment.

'That's not the case, Moira. If it wasn't such a big day tomorrow, I'd definitely go – I'd like to meet her teachers and put her case forward, support her, ask the questions she needs answered. It's just a timing thing. I can't not be there at the pub whilst the work's going on. I've got to organise everyone. I've got everything riding on this new business, and we have no income while we're closed, so the turnaround is really tight. I can't dick the guys around – they have to stay on track otherwise the paint literally won't be dry by opening night.'

My voice is starting to crack. I can't believe Moira thinks I would just not show up for Ruby without good reason. But I can't skip tomorrow. It's not just my reputation at stake, it's Danny's too. What kind of partner would he think I was if I was already too busy to help? The pub's not even open yet.

But Moira's not having it, and she strikes her hand against the door.

'I wish you'd thought about that before you went and put stars in her eyes. Now she thinks everything is on the up. She thinks she's going to pass her exams and get into art college and do all the things she wants to and have a great life altogether.' She is shaking her head like these things are catastrophic, and for the first time it dawns on me that Moira doesn't want Ruby to succeed. She wants her to stay like she is, unhappy and unfulfilled but close by, at home, within easy reach. Poor Ruby. You need the people around you to love you enough to let you go and live the life you want – even if it means moving away and leaving them behind. I feel my heart swell in my chest.

Moira is jabbering on, pointing a sharp-nailed finger in the air. 'I warned her that reality doesn't work out that way. "Prepare to be disappointed," I said. I told her not to get her hopes up, that that's not real life.'

I open the door as wide as it will go and step square in front of Moira. If I did put stars in Ruby's eyes, then wonderful. Now I've got to make sure she keeps reaching for them.

'No, Moira. You're wrong. It *could* be Ruby's real life. It could be her reality if she keeps believing in herself and working hard towards her dream the way she is.'

Moira tuts at me and rolls her eyes. A flashback to James's eye-rolling sends fury boiling through me. How dare people put limitations on others? How dare Moira or James or anyone else determine what is or isn't possible for people to achieve?

I raise my hand to halt Moira's riposte.

'Tomorrow. At Ruby's school. I'll be there.'

'Oh, so you can make it now.' She cocks a disbelieving eyebrow.

I'll have to call Danny and explain, but somehow I know he's going to understand. It's Ruby's future at stake here. I've got to tread carefully – her dreams are fragile. The slightest setback could tear them apart. If showing up for her makes the difference, then that's what I've got to do. It's funny: I'd never have trusted James to take over a big project like I'm asking Danny to do. Even though I haven't known him that long, he understands what it means to me. He won't let me down. We've got to trust each other now that we're partners. That's how it has to be.

'I'll work it out. Just tell me when and where.'

'St Augustine's, just off Parnell Street. The appointment is at midday; expect a bit of a journey to get there. There are always roadworks, traffic jams on that side of town. And don't get me started on the parking: complete nightmare.'

Great. Operation Rosie Munroe's is only just getting going, and tomorrow I'll be exactly where I never thought I'd be again: sitting in a classroom. But this time I'll be on the other side of the desk, fighting for the most important student I've ever had.

CHAPTER NINETEEN

'Let me put you in the picture, Ms Dooley.' Ruby's head teacher, Mr Byrne, cracks his hard-boiled egg against the desk. 'The case of Ruby O'Shea is far from straightforward.' He picks away the fragments of shell and piles them up into a little mound in front of him. 'Now, I'll be frank with you,' he whispers, turning in his chair to check that no one is behind him. Satisfied that the coast is clear, he continues. 'After everything that happened last year, we thought we'd seen the end of Ruby...'

'I don't follow, Mr Byrne,' I say, tired of his conspiratorial vagueness.

'She's a promiscuous sort of girl anyhow – you can always spot them a mile off – and she had a boyfriend called Dylan. He was a complete moron, involved with petty crime and gangs and the like. Anyway, she got involved with the wrong crowd and her attendance, her attitude, the standard of her school work slipped; she went completely off the rails.' He opens a file in front of him, shaking his head. 'An absolute nightmare on every level. Then her grandmother shows up shouting the odds, wants everything brushed under the carpet – forget anything ever happened and can we all please back off and leave them alone.'

He pops the whole egg into his mouth. I wince before I can help myself.

'Why would she do that?'

He opens his eggy mouth to reply and throws his arms up in the air.

'Because she is a total nutjob!' He counts on his fingers. 'She couldn't give a toss about anyone but herself. She's banned from here; she went for me at a parents' evening when I told her that she could be fined for Ruby's truancy – launched herself at me like a ninja, wrapped her hands around my neck. Absolute maniac.'

'I'm sorry to hear that,' I say, as I consider how much courage it must have taken for Ruby to trust me. The poor girl had cried out for help and nobody had listened, nobody had cared what was going on in her life.

'What's the problem now? Why did you need to see me today?'

Mr Byrne shakes his head as he brushes the broken eggshell to the edge of the table and into his cupped hand.

'Ruby's back at square one. Her grades have slipped. She won't pass her exams at this rate, and then what kind of future will she have? Probably not a very nice one.' He pauses and locks eyes with me.

'Don't get me wrong. I like Ruby. She's a good girl in her own way, smart at times too. But it's just one drama after another. It's exhausting. I'm exhausted.' His shoulders slump low in resignation. 'She seems to have given up and doesn't pay attention to her studies any more. It's unlikely that things will ever get better for her if she carries on this way. What happens next is anyone's guess. So, some friendly advice from me to you: get her to buck her ideas up, or she has no future.'

I stay seated, trying to absorb everything he has told me. The school have given up on her – they're just counting down the days until she's not their problem any more. The lunch bell rings and Mr Byrne stands to end the meeting.

'I can tell by the look on your face that you don't believe me. Fine – you think you can do a better job? Be my guest.' He slides his chair underneath the table and walks me out of the office.

I text Danny and tell him that I may be a little while longer, because first I need to find Ruby and think of a way to tell her that she needs to pull her finger out, get the work done and pass her exams. And then I've just got to wait and see if anything I say will make a blind bit of difference.

As I turn in at the gate of the house, I spot her sitting on the steps, sketching in her folder. I slow down and take my time opening the gate and thinking about what I am going to say to her. She's already so far away from the angry girl I found here in a drunken heap not so long ago. She's moving in the right direction, she's made so much progress; I want to tell her to keep going, to keep working, that it will all pay off in the long run, but the long run seems so very far away when you're seventeen and surrounded by obstacles. And I also know that it doesn't work when someone simply tells you what you need to do or what you should be thinking. It needs to come from inside, a desire to do it for yourself.

'Hey there,' I say, sitting beside her on the step. 'Just been to your school, met Mr Byrne.' She blinks quickly and doesn't smile. 'I got an idea about what it might be like there.' She looks up at me this time. 'The good news is he still thinks you have time to turn it around.'

Ruby shakes her head and drops her pencil. 'Why should I? They don't help, they don't like me, they can't wait for me to leave and get out of their way.'

'Whether that's the case or not isn't important. There will always be people standing in your way, trying to block you, and there will always be people standing up for you, fighting your corner, encouraging you and wanting to help you along. So it's important that you pay attention to the right people.'

I pick up her pencil and hand it back to her. 'Ruby, as you grow up, you are told the world is fixed, that things are the way they are supposed to be and your main goal should be just to live your life according to the rules. Try not to make too much noise, or cause too much fuss, or draw attention to yourself. Don't bash into the walls or break anything. Try to be good, stay safe and save a little money.'

I swallow hard and try to pick my next words carefully, so that she really hears me, really understands what I'm trying to say.

'That's a very limited way to live. Life can be much broader once you understand one simple fact: everything around you was made up by people who were no smarter than you, no better than you; it's just that they were really brave. And if you can find your courage, you can change whatever you need to, you can be in charge of your life and you can live the biggest, boldest life you can dream of. Once you learn that, you're never quite the same again.'

She looks up at me. 'Is that what happened to you?' she asks.

'Yes,' I tell her. 'It's what is still happening to me.'

She nods, closes her eyes and hugs her legs a moment, then stands up and stretches her arms into the sky.

'Right, I'm going inside. I've got some studying to do.'

And I think about telling her that I'm already so proud of her. But I can see from the funny little look on her face that she already knows.

CHAPTER TWENTY

Tonight is the night: the grand opening.

A wave of adrenalin ripples through me as I think about everything that has happened, good and not so good, to bring me to this point. Standing behind this counter, on the cusp of a new career, is a huge adventure. But there is no denying it, it is also a big risk. A very big, expensive, public risk. I've woken up in a cold sweat every night this week, panicking myself with negative thoughts. What if no one shows up? Or if loads of people show up but we run out of beer? Or gin? Or ice? Or staff? What if the toilet gets blocked, or overflows, or another fight breaks out and someone gets hurt and the police are called, or one of the other ten thousand things that could go wrong tonight happens? I feel like I've not slept a wink, fighting off these doomsday scenarios that haunt me the moment I close my eyes at night.

And I know it's not all unfounded fear. Any or all of these things could happen. The closest thing I've ever done to this is serving tea and sandwiches with my mother's church group.

Holy shit, this is terrifying. I grab the counter and try to channel Rosie Munroe. Fearless and brimming with self-belief. A woman with purpose, with vision. That's how I need to feel right now. And I *am* feeling it; I just need to anchor it, to stay calm and keep my head together and not let myself get overawed at how this is really coming together. Because if this is anything, it's pretty awesome.

Danny carries in a crate of beer and starts stocking the fridge. 'What's wrong? You don't look yourself. Are you okay?'

'I'm so nervous.'

He puts his hands on my shoulders. 'Nothing to worry about. We've booked Supanova! These guys are the hottest ticket around. They are going to bring a flock of punters with them – tonight could seriously put us on the map as the best new live music venue in the city.'

'Or the worst.' I clutch at my chest. I'm the most nervous I've ever been in my life. 'What was I thinking? How can we possibly do this? If Colm couldn't do it, why on earth did I think we could pull it off?'

'We are going to pull it off because we've broken our backs getting this place sorted out, and it looks incredible. We've put in the work. We're ready. Colm stopped trying; he stopped believing. We *are* trying and we *do* believe. It's going to be sensational, I promise you. I won't let you down.'

I nod along and start helping him with the bottles, trying to take deep breaths.

He throws a lemon at me and laughs. 'Do you feel like you need the toilet more than normal?'

'Yes! How did you know? But I can't go. Do you think something is wrong? Oh, I can't be sick tonight, of all nights!'

'Stage fright, Evelyn. That's all it is. I used to get it all the time when I first started performing. But instead of feeling nervous, you just say to yourself three times, "I'm excited. I'm excited. I'm excited."'

I nod. 'Okay.'

'Say it now. We'll do it together.'

I slow my breathing and together we say the words aloud. 'I'm excited. I'm excited. I'm excited.'

'How do you feel now?'

I smile at him. 'Excited?'

'Good, now let's get this show on the road.'

*

The clock strikes eight and I begin watching the door. Couples and clusters of very cool-looking young people start to gather outside. I imagine them following their GPSs all the way across town and then texting their friends to say, yeah, we're here, we think this is the place, the one on every poster, flyer in town alongside complete social media bombardment thanks to Ruby's relentless (and brilliant) digital campaign. This is the place all the hype is about.

I run my fingers through my hair, muttering to myself, 'I'm excited. I'm excited. I am feckin' excited…'

A gaggle of girls pour in through the door: our first customers. They are laughing and giggling, all of them wearing conical cardboard party hats. It's Tara and her aircrew mates.

Tara spots me behind the bar and starts waving and bouncing up and down. After a flurry of hugs and kisses, she introduces me to the girls. 'It's Gemma's birthday, so we thought we'd come and support you! Rent-a-crowd are us!'

Oh how I appreciate her lovely intentions. She's the greatest. I line them up twelve tequila slammers on the house.

'To your new adventure.' Tara winks before we both lick the salt and throw back our shots.

The place slowly starts to fill up. I weave my way across the dance floor, through Tara's crowd of girls, and slip into the ladies' toilet for a quick breather before it gets too busy. Happily, the end cubicle is free – always my favourite – and I turn the latch on the door and have a well-earned sit down.

I think it's the tequila that did it: finally helped me loosen up in every sense. I rest my head against the toilet-roll dispenser, grateful for the moment of solitude, a chance to compose myself before the big night sucks me in and I learn whether we will sink or swim.

I hear voices outside. And Tara's shrill laughter.

'The thing with my sister is that she always puts others first. She always does the right thing over what's actually right for her. Let me give you an example: marrying James O'Connor. Talk about a disaster waiting to happen.'

OMG. She's talking about me.

I stand up quietly and press my ear against the cubicle door.

'Evelyn was always the quiet, head-down, books-under-her-arm type at school. She could easily have been the big sister I hated for being so good at everything: good at school, good at home, everything tidy and underlined, good at listening to old people tell long stories without wincing or shuffling, good at always knowing the cues to offer a cup of tea.'

'Golden girl?' I recognise the Spanish accent; it's Tara's flatmate, Inez.

'Exactly. So it'd be easy to hate her if you were a complete jealous bastard. But nobody did because that's just what she's like – she sees the gaps in things, she pays attention to cracks and sees where the need is. That's what my father used to tell us – Evelyn sees the cracks, and that's a gift; sure it's through the cracks that the light gets in.'

'So she saw the need in James?' offers Inez.

'Exactly, he lured her in and then he trapped her,' says Tara.

I hear a flush next door. No! Don't stop this conversation. I want to hear more! I never knew Tara felt this way, saw me this way. I knew she wasn't crazy about James, but I had no idea she felt he had trapped me.

'Although they were in the same school year, they hardly crossed paths until Dad hired James for some building work one summer. That was where it started. Evelyn made bulging ham salad sandwiches and hot flasks of dark tea for him; she'd hop up on the wall and chat to him as he plastered and painted. The next thing we knew he was taking her out to gigs and for meals, and that seemed to seal the deal. They were a couple from then on. He never let her out of his sight. It was all concerts and drinks with his friends, and then weekends away and beach holidays abroad. All her own friends fell away, as did all her own plans. She became James's support act. Everything revolved around him – do you want to come to Dublin for a night out? I'll have to ask James. If she saw a dress in a shop window, she'd have to text him. Someone asked her a question in a crowd, her eyes would dart a look at him. It was like a secret language of approval, like a choirgirl miming the words in case she sang the wrong ones.'

'Control freak,' says Inez.

'Yeah, if there's such a thing as a really lazy control freak. That's James O'Connor.'

I hear the taps running. I kind of want that to be the end now. I'm shocked. I never thought of James as a control freak. I thought of him as a bit of a drifter, but with the right direction I thought he had a good heart. I thought he was there because he loved me, not because he wanted to control me.

They continue. I can hear lipsticks clicking open.

'James set up his building business while Evelyn went to university. But he bought her a car so she'd have no excuse not to live at home and see him every day. I didn't like that.'

I didn't really like that either to be fair, but I thought it was a good idea at the time. And then our lovely dad died. And I suppose in a way we were all relieved that I was sticking around, so Mum wasn't on her own. Tara had already moved to Dublin to start her training, how could I let mum lose everyone all at once?

'I wanted Evelyn to experience student life properly; to get drunk and meet new people and go to house parties and wake up on a strange sofa beside someone she didn't know. Stuff that would broaden her world, bring her out of herself, show her that she didn't always have to be Evelyn the good daughter/student/

girlfriend/tea-bringer. I suspect James had the same idea and put things in place so that good Evelyn would stay exactly as she was.'

'So how do you think she is doing? Now that it's all over?'

Yes, how *am* I doing?

'I don't know. She'll give you the shirt off her back or her last chip, but when it comes to accepting good old-fashioned assistance herself, she's at a loss.'

'I think she will do fine. She has a sister who loves her, and we can achieve anything with love and support. What's that you always say? "Begin where you are, and then reach for the stars." She will be okay, we will make it so.'

Thank you, darling Inez! is what I want to call out, but I keep quiet. I have to do this on my own. I have to make it so by myself.

And with that, I hear them zipping up their make-up bags, and they are gone.

I will never let Tara know that I heard her speak like this about me; she would be mortified, but she'd probably also tell me more. Neither of which I want to happen. Because that chapter in my life is over, that girl is gone.

I leave the loos and grab my chance to gather the team out back. Ruby's brought some friends in tonight to help out, poaching them from their other casual glass-collecting jobs for our big night. She's in charge of floor service, and I've got to say, she's done a great job so far. All five of her friends are dressed in our Rosie Munroe's red, white and black T-shirts, hair pulled back off their faces, apron pockets full of pens, notepads at the ready.

'Right, guys,' I begin. 'Tonight is our big chance. It's make or break really. If all goes to plan, then we'll have broken into the scene and we can start booking bands a couple of nights a week, which should see us making this dream a reality – putting Rosie Munroe's back on the map and a new lease of life for all of us.

Equally, if it doesn't go to plan, whether it's the drink, customer service or something else that falls short, we're going to find it difficult, if not impossible, to claw our way back. It's a tough industry; people have lots of choices and little time or interest in revisiting something that doesn't deliver. We've got one shot tonight to really go for it.'

Danny puts his hand in the middle of the circle. 'Remember we're a team. Let's reach for the stars, people. If you see someone struggling, take a breath, step towards them and ask if you can help. Stay cool. And most of all, enjoy it. We're here for a good time, and so are our customers, so soak it up, try your best. Feel excited; we're lucky to be a part of this. Who knows where tonight will lead us, right?'

We hug, high-five and slap each other's backs, smiling our determination to make this the greatest night Rosie Munroe's has had in over twenty years.

By quarter to ten, the place is absolutely packed. Christy is standing by the double doors as a very friendly bouncer, welcoming the crowd, directing them in, bantering happily with everyone in the queue that is now snaking around the corner. Colm is behind the bar, smiling widely as he serves drink after drink to the mass of people.

'Sound check and lighting sorted,' shouts Danny as he leans across the bar. I can barely hear him over the excited chatter of our swelling crowds. 'All we need is for Supanova to lug their gear on stage and we're ready to go. Are they out back?'

Um… no. There is no one out back. I shake my head and look across the sea of faces. 'I haven't seen them at all. I presumed they were already setting up with you.'

There is a hint of panic in my voice, and Danny's instruction to stay cool is evaporating very quickly. No band? What the hell?

They have *one* job: show up and play. And they haven't even got the first part of that right. Where are they?

I feel my stomach double over on itself. 'This can't be happening, right? You definitely booked them?'

Danny is trying to smile and assuage my fears, but I can see a slight alarm in his eyes as he searches the crowd for five dishevelled-looking band members, complete with instruments, spray-on black jeans and no sense of time or direction.

'Let's give it five more minutes. They may just be running late. Leave it with me.'

I don't like leaving things with people. Especially things that have all my money and reputation riding on them. The stage is still in darkness. A restlessness has overtaken our crowd, and I see their furrowed brows and anxious checking of phones. Shouldn't something be happening by now? Ruby and the others thread in between the seated and standing drinkers, but rather than taking orders, they are being stopped now by customers with frowning faces and open palms. *What time is the music starting? What's the delay? I came here to see Supanova. What the hell is going on?*

I wish I knew.

I don't know what to do. But I'm going to have to do *something*. We're minutes away from losing this crowd. And if we lose this crowd, we've lost our whole venture. This won't be the home of new music; it's not the home of any music – just confused whispers and enquiring murmurs. I'll have to take the stage myself. Explain what's happened. Just tell them straight that we're sorry, the band haven't shown up, and… offer them all a free drink? As reasonable as that sounds, there must be nearly four hundred people in here right now. I'm already in minus figures after the refurb and all the staff I've got to pay tonight. I can't absorb another loss like that.

Danny said to give it five minutes. That was thirty minutes ago.

Right. I push up the counter hatch. I'll need to get on stage and offer up a grovelling apology. Let's hope they understand. Or at least let's hope they don't throw anything at me.

And if they do throw stuff, please let it not be glass.

'They're still not here,' Ruby says, looking at her watch. 'What shall we tell everyone?'

My heart rate is high. 'No sign of them at all?'

She shakes her head.

I ask her to take over at the bar and start battling my way through the crowd. Why did I ever think we could do this? It's too big, too much, too risky. I am feet away, the feeling of dread rising like acid bile into my mouth, when suddenly the lights go up and a figure walks onto the stage.

It's Danny. He must be about to break the news himself.

I stop in my tracks and take in everything we worked so hard to save. We came so close. I look around, breathing in the heat of our packed house. Our beautiful lighting, our red-painted walls with gold skirting. Our varnished counter and floorboards, our gorgeous uniformed staff. And, of course, our empty stage.

We really did nearly make it.

Up until this very moment, I believed.

What happens next is not going to be pleasant. The crowd will be seriously pissed off. We have no other bands, no other line-up. We put all our trust and money in Supanova. I glance back to Ruby behind the bar and realise that we should have told the staff first; they will be the ones bearing the brunt of the customer angst. I have no idea what Danny plans to say, but however it comes out, the punters won't be happy.

Danny adjusts the height of the microphone and taps on it. 'Welcome to Rosie Munroe's,' he announces, giving a small wave to the crowd.

The drinkers nudge each other, the roar of conversation fades to a hush and they all turn their faces up towards him and settle in to listen; they know this drill, this is what they came for, and boy, are they ready.

Danny pulls up a stool and sits down.

'I'd like to thank everyone for coming tonight. Saturday nights are precious; you work hard, you want to spend your time and your money on something worthwhile – and you chose us. Evelyn and myself and all the staff are really happy that you did, and I want to say from the bottom of our hearts that we appreciate it, thank you.'

He's working up to telling them, trying to get them on side before he delivers the big blow. I bury my face in my hands, peeking through my fingers at him up on the stage. I hope nobody physically assaults him.

But then he grabs his guitar from the stand and positions it on his thigh. He glances over the audience several times, but he doesn't spot me. At least I think it's me he's looking for.

He clears his throat, curls his fingers around the neck of the guitar and closes his eyes for a moment. A hush descends.

He starts to finger-pick, and then a shadow lifts from his eyes and he's smiling, like he's excited about what's going to happen. His smile lights up his face and illuminates the entire room – at least that's what it seems like to me. He looks incredible.

'So, a bit of a surprise for you first.' He looks into the audience again, and this time he finds me straight away. 'Because I love a surprise.' He winks at me, and my heart crashes to the floor.

He's going to play.

I can't smile or wave or nod back at him. I'm too nervous to move. I love Danny's set outside, but these guys have travelled here to see a professional band. Are they going to be okay with a busker's playlist? Please let this work, whatever he has up his sleeve, please let it make everyone realise how talented and caring and lovely he is. I want them to clap him and whoop and appreciate him and fall a little bit in love with him. Just like me.

'Some of you might remember my brother Rory and me from various gigs around the place.'

'The Musketeers!' someone in the crowd shouts, and a dawning seems to ripple through the rest, heads bobbing and nodding. Spontaneous applause erupts. Danny blushes red.

'Thank you. I appreciate that. Well, the thing is, there's just one lone Musketeer these days. Tonight is the first time I've played on stage without him – and I'm not going to lie to you guys, it feels strange.' His gaze finds mine again. 'But we've promised you a night you'll never forget, and that's exactly what you're going to get.'

He plays the opening chords of something I don't recognise. And I realise that it's not something anyone will recognise. He's playing his own composition, an original.

Oh my God, he must be shitting himself. I am so proud of him, all I want to do is wrap my arms around his neck and hold his face in my hands and tell him so. But I remain completely immobile as he sings his own words to his own music, keeping his focus on his fingers as they work the strings.

We never knew a time
When we did not share
Our birth, our day, our years
Our then, our now, our dreams, our fears
We were us and we – not I and me
We were them and they – not him and he
We were their and theirs – not my or his
Once forever was not mine, but ours

As I listen, I clutch my hand to my chest, blown away by the beauty that he can create all by himself with just a few words and a voice and an instrument. It's mesmerising. For the entire length of the song I barely move, barely breathe, afraid I'll miss a beat.

When you died you took with you our shared, our special we
Leaving behind this lone Musketeer
A lost and singular me

The sheer honesty and raw emotion in his expression, in his entire body, has transformed this room into a hushed, charged, sacred space. My hands are pressed against my breastbone; the whole place is suspended in a collective moment of breathlessness. And then a slow, lone clap begins beside me, a distinguished older gentleman with white-silver hair, wearing a black leather jacket. The rest of the crowd join in, and I look around me, at men shaking their heads, running their hands through their hair, women dabbing their eyes and holding fingers under their noses to bite back the urge to cry.

Everything and nothing has happened, all inside a couple of moments.

He did it. He did it for us. He stepped outside his fear, exposing himself in the most revealing way to tell his truth, to share it in order to save our night. To save our chance of a future together at Rosie Munroe's. And if I'm completely honest with myself, if I step outside my fear of uncertainty and decide to expose myself in the most revealing way, just as he did, I know what I'll find. I'll find that I may be falling in love. It feels like he has taken me over at every level. He hasn't just swept me off my feet, but swept me away, wiped me out. I want to go to him so badly.

'Wow,' whispers Ruby. Her eyes are glued to the stage, just like mine. Just like every other pair of eyes in the room.

Singing his own material, for the first time without his brother, in front of a brand-new crowd is something I never expected. It's something I would never have asked him to do. Stepping up that way, taking such a risk, revealing the most vulnerable, raw side of himself to a room full of strangers, the drunk, the crazed and the critical amongst them, is one of the most amazing things anyone has ever done for me.

I'm shaking my head, unable to get it into my mind that this man is willingly mine. He's perfect and caring and beautiful and talented and good and… And just as all this is running through my brain, he looks at me. Our eyes lock, and I don't look away. He's smiling, but I'm frozen in shock.

Ruby shoves me in the shoulder. 'The band are here. What do I tell them?'

'Tell them to get up on that stage and bring the house down.'

And that's exactly what they do.

'What a night. Seriously, what a NIGHT!' I usher out the last revved-up customers, who are singing our praises and promising to spread the word. I bolt the door behind them and collapse into the corner seat.

'Leave the rest of the clean-up until the morning,' I tell Danny as he collects the last few bottles from the counter. 'After a night like that, I think we deserve a rest.' I tip my head back and take in the new smell hanging in the air. It's heavy, tinged with sour beer and body heat, and I breathe it in in gulps. Because that's the smell of our grand opening success. That's the smell of a packed house and a busy bar and a raucous, dancing, laughing, jumping-up-and-down crowd who spilt their drinks on the floor and wrapped their arms around the sweaty necks of their friends.

To me, Rosie Munroe's has never smelt so good.

Danny cracks open two cold bottles of beer for us and slides in beside me. 'It was incredible. And check this out.' He flicks a business card over to me. 'Supanova's agent asked us to give him a ring with some new dates and they'll work around us. They're touring big-time at the moment, UK and Europe for the next two months, but after that they want Rosie Munroe's to be their home-town gig.' He takes a sip of his beer and settles back into his seat. 'They loved it all – the acoustics, the ambience, the old-school intimacy. This is huge. He's writing a glowing review of the place for their website tomorrow, so expect the word to start spreading. They've got a massive following.'

He raises his bottle to me. 'Congratulations, Evelyn, you did it. We wouldn't be here without your vision and your bossy, ballsy, go-hard-or-go-home attitude.'

'*We* did it. The two of us, together.' I clink my bottle to his. 'Thank you.'

'Your song. Did you write that?'

He nods. 'I always saw me and Rory as two halves of the same person, and I guess I've drifted a lot without him. Not really knowing what direction to go in, not trusting what I should do next; I'd always just followed his lead. So until you came along, I guess I was just hanging out at the crossroads, literally playing my guitar on the corner, stalling and trying to get out of making any decisions. But I've got to make those decisions now. And being on the stage tonight by myself, singing my own song, I guess that was another step towards that.'

He swallows a moment and then nudges my elbow.

'And then this crazy country girl shows up with plans and visions and checklists. And that's how it happened.'

I shift up in my seat and meet his gaze. 'Every time I think I've started to figure you out, you go and do something that completely surprises me.'

His fingers tiptoe towards mine. And keep stepping up across my wrist, along the soft inside part of my arm, right up to my necklace. He traces his fingertip along the thin silver chain, my skin quivering under his touch.

'Fancy a sleepover?' I ask him.

He leans towards me, takes my hand in his and raises it to his lips. He closes his eyes and brushes his lips against my fingers, then, holding my gaze, he presses his cheek against my hand.

'You sure that's what you want?' he asks.

'Yes,' I say, my breath catching. 'It's what I really, really want.'

And we scramble out of the double front doors of Rosie Munroe's as fast as if the place was on fire.

CHAPTER TWENTY-ONE

I'm awake but I don't want to open my eyes yet. Danny is still asleep, right beside me. I lie on my back and I can feel his breath on my skin, one of his arms behind my neck, the other wrapped around my waist. If I open my eyes, I might rush this moment, push it forward too fast and lose all its gorgeous, warm, sexy deliciousness.

The scent of him, like soap and salt on these fresh white sheets. I just want to stay here, bask in this. I listen to the rhythm of his breathing and feel the warmth of his skin against mine.

Last night was the best night of my life.

'Evelyn,' he murmurs.

'Yes.'

'Good,' he says. 'You're real. I didn't want to open my eyes in case it was a dream.'

'Me too.' I smile. 'Shall we open on three?'

'Okay. One, two...' and we both blink our eyes open, turning to each other, smiling our most heartfelt smiles. He gently presses his thumb against my temple, smoothing a stray tendril of hair. 'You are lovely. Last night was...' he blows out his cheeks, 'lovely.'

I nod my agreement. Having only ever been with one man in my entire life, I was nervous, but there was no need. Nothing short of excitement and elation took over. Danny is a kisser. He kissed every inch of me, soft and wet and long and hard. After all this time, after wanting him and watching him and resisting him for so long, to give in, to give myself over to him came as such a liberating relief. I felt that freedom, the openness, with every nerve in my body – with every kiss, with every whisper, with every shudder. And when the time came for us to get even closer, it felt the most natural next step in the world. Like darkness fading into light, like the shoreline meeting the water, like a bird taking flight, at long last.

He checks the clock by the bedside. 'It's just gone nine. If we head in to do the clear-up in an hour or so, we'll be ready to reopen at midday. Sound good, boss?'

'Sounds perfect,' I tell him.

'And how about coffee, or tea? Bacon, eggs, pancakes?'

'Breakfast in bed? Even more surprises, Danny Foy.' I nuzzle in to him and run my fingers through his hair. 'Is this what life's going be like if I stick with you? Surprises every day?'

He smiles. 'Really? You want to stick around a smelly old busker like me?'

I push myself up on my elbow. 'Don't do yourself down.' I lean forward and kiss him on the forehead. 'You are a beautiful man. A beautiful, generous, talented man and a hell of a kisser. I think I could get very fond of sticking around you.'

He raises a playful eyebrow. 'Well I can't say I'd object to waking up to this little pep talk every morning.'

And with that he slides his hands over my body with a look in his eye that makes me want him all over again.

And again.

And maybe again after that.

CHAPTER TWENTY-TWO

If Danny's playlist reflects his mood, then I think I must be doing something right. It's mellow and easy but also sexy and new; high, happy notes with lyrics full of love and cheery playfulness. And it suits me to listen, to bask in this sound as my days play out. I could listen and watch him and sneak kisses in the cellar and brush behind him and make jokes and hold his hand and work alongside him, touching distance from him, in our beautiful bar every day of my life. He is the best partner I could have. He's super-organised, knows exactly what stock we have, keeps on top of the orders, the invoices and receipts; and he is brilliant with the customers – he greets everyone with a smile, and people often stay for much more than one drink if he catches them in conversation.

We've attracted a bit of a cult following. Tara managed to get Rosie Munroe's a mention in the 'Must Visit' section of the inflight magazine, so pretty much every passenger who's taken the time to read it has popped in for a drink. Even Mum's going to come and stay for a few days once her parish trip to Rome is out of the way. We've had to take on new staff and our music calendar is now fully booked for the next six months. The live gigs every Friday and Saturday more than cover our expenses for the rest of the week, so all the midweek trade is profit.

Colm's not visited for a while, which is a positive thing because he is using his new-found time to read and visit old friends and look after his health a bit more, walking and sleeping and eating decent meals. Christy still sits at the bar every day; he's in his element giving informal history talks to the tourists. He loves recounting the old stories, showing them photographs, answering their questions. It's been good for him too, because it's made him lay off the whiskey. Says it fogs his memory and makes him slur his words; no good for a social historian! Instead I leave a pot of coffee warm for him on the side, so if he gets the urge, all he has to do is lean over the counter and help himself. So far, so good. For me, seeing the place transformed from an unloved little pub to a thriving social hub has brought enormous pride and satisfaction. I want to stay here like this forever.

The clock strikes eleven and I throw the double doors of the new and improved Rosie Munroe's open wide. I turn back in the doorway with my hands on my hips, watching the sunlight flood in, gorgeous buttery sunshine reflecting off the mirrors, the shiny brass fixtures and the varnished darkwood floor. The stained-glass panels give a dappled quality to the air, and the fresh scent of hot roasted coffee and grilled maple bacon fills the air. Some customers have started to file in already; the office crowd will follow soon after that, and then we'll not get a chance to sit down until we ring the bell and call closing time.

I carry the chalkboard outside. Usually I don't know what I'm going to write until I crouch down in front of it, but today is different. Today is my father's birthday, so in memory of him I'm going to share his heart, his thoughts and his advice with the world. I inscribe carefully in my best handwriting:

'Set your sights on the sky and reach for the stars.'
Quote courtesy of the late, great William Dooley

I hear Danny calling me from inside, so I stand up, send a little kiss skywards and return behind the bar, where I belong.

CHAPTER TWENTY-THREE

The new day begins with a text from Mum.

Stay dry, bad weather promised in Dublin. Saw it on news. Storms here. What letter are we up to now with the storms? G? H? We'll be looking for new names again soon at this rate. Hope all well besides. Love you xx

She's not wrong. It's pouring down with rain this morning, and I'm drenched when I get to the pub despite the umbrella Danny insisted I take with me.

It doesn't take me long to finish off the rest of the clear-up from the night before, and soon I settle into my own lovely landlady routine: kettle on, music on, strike up the fire and get ready for the day ahead, whatever it may bring.

As I sit in front of the fireplace with my warming mug of coffee, I feel a funny kind of shiver and the hairs stand up on the back of my neck. I snuggle down into my sweater, throw another log on and double-check that all the windows are sealed shut as the rain lashes down even harder outside.

Today might be quiet due to this weather; people may choose to stay indoors rather than brave the elements. Or it could be the complete opposite: droves of people shaking their wet hair and shopping bags might run in for respite as they make their way from place to place. Just like I did on that very first day, when I took a turn through that double doorway, frazzled and tired, not realising that I was stepping into the place where I feel I belong more than anywhere else in the world.

I hold my coffee up to my face, breathing in its milky warmth. How lucky I was to turn that corner. How grateful I am to be here. Never in my wildest imagination did I think that this was the way my story would unfold. If I hadn't acted on my unhappiness with James, I'd never have set out on my own. If I hadn't acted on Tara's offer, I'd never have made it to Dublin. If I'd never convinced Colm to give me a chance, who knows what I'd be doing. And that makes me so happy and proud, because without the changes that happened in my life, I'd never have learnt what I could do, and what I really want. Throwing everything up in the air and watching it fall back into place has renewed my faith in myself, in my own capabilities, and maybe even in Colm's idea of there being a master plan after all.

Kneeling down at the hearth, I prod at the fire with the big ancient poker and wait for the tinder to really take light and fill the room with a great big crackling blaze. A cold, whistling wind blows in again, but I can't work out where it's coming from; there's no sign of a draught that I can see. *Someone's walked over your grave*, my mother would say. Well I think I can rule that out, considering the week I've had. I couldn't possibly feel more alive. I didn't know it could be like this, I didn't know I could feel this way. My heart twists in my chest and I shake my head. I can't believe I was afraid of getting into something new. Something new was *exactly* what I needed. And it feels wonderful, like I'm really on my way.

I hear a tap on the front window and look up to see Danny waving at me from outside. He's soaked to the skin, which must mean that he gave me his one and only umbrella. I rush to open the door for him and give him a peck on the cheek, then set about making him a coffee too.

By the time I look up at the clock, it's past midday, yet there's no sign of Christy. In all the time I've been here, he's marched in through those doors, paper under arm, by twelve every single day.

But not today.

Danny emerges from the cellar with a new barrel to change over.

'It's odd that Christy's late. Do you think he's okay?' I ask.

Danny twists the seal and attacks the pipes. I'm so grateful he does this job, as I hate the cellar; it gives me the creeps.

He shrugs. 'It's really wet out there; he might have just decided to wait until it eases up before he comes down.'

Almost on cue, the front door flings open with the force of the wind, and there is Christy, breathless, hunched and soaked through to the skin, leaning on the door frame.

We run to him and Danny throws his arms around his back to scoop him in as I pull against the wind to shut the doors behind him. We sit him by the fire, take his wet coat and cap and drape a blanket over his shoulders. I make him a hot whiskey with lemon, cloves and plenty of sugar. Christy doesn't say a word.

This is not normal. I dart a look at Danny and he pinches his lips together. Something has happened to the old man, and whatever it is, it has knocked him for six. He hasn't even looked up yet, so deep is his shock. There isn't any sign of injury or bleeding, so I'm certain he hasn't fallen or been hit by a car. So what is it? What's so terrible that it has rendered him a ghost of himself?

Danny turns down the music and we sit either side of him.

'Are you all right, Christy? Has something happened?' I ask gently, tilting my head to try and meet his eyes.

He shuts his.

I reach for his hand and feel his long, bony fingers in mine. He places his other hand on top and raises his head, looking straight into the fire. 'Colm.'

I nod and wait, glancing over to Danny. He is biting his bottom lip; he knows that whatever comes next isn't going be good news. Fresh tears pool in Christy's eyes.

'Colm's dead. He had surgery, kept it quiet and told no one, thinking he could just check himself in and out, no fuss. But his heart wasn't strong enough and he went under but never woke up.' He closes his eyes and dips his chin to his chest. I squeeze his hands, but they stay rigid in mine. 'Never regained consciousness. That's what the doctor said.'

I look to Danny; he stands and bolts the lock on the front door.

We sit and try to shoulder the weight of the news. The suddenness. The finality. I knew Colm wasn't well, but I never expected this. I don't think he expected it either. And why would he? He thought he was going in for a straightforward operation. My efforts to keep a dignified silence collapse as the sheer shock of the whole thing makes me dissolve into tears.

'Oh Christy, I'm so sorry. Poor Colm. Anything you need, we are here for you. If you need us to contact people, make arrangements, take care of you or anyone else – we are here.'

I look up to Danny, conscious that I've just spoken on behalf of both of us, committed him to a level of help that he might not want to give. But he steps up to Christy and places his hand on his shoulder.

'Anything, Christy. I lost my brother. I know there are no words for the pain. If we can help you, let us.'

For the first time, Christy's watery eyes leave the fire and he looks up.

'Thank you. Thank you both. This place is all I've got left.'

CHAPTER TWENTY-FOUR

I hate funerals.

Hundreds of people show up to say goodbye, to pay their final respects to Colm. As he had no family left, it falls to Danny and me to stand either side of Christy and shake the mourners' hands, thank them for coming, accept their sympathies.

A crowd a hundred deep follows the wreathed hearse through the street. When we reach Rosie's, the car stops. We all stop. And in a moment of collective silence, we somehow let Colm say goodbye to his place in the world. The place where his life began and ended, where he spent every single one of his years on earth. And now he is gone, just like every one of his predecessors. But still the building remains, the pub stays as it has done through the ages, surviving despite deaths and wars and recessions and constant change and fluctuation. Rosie's still stands, a testament to his life, to his friendships, to his memory.

The moment passes and it is time for the hearse to resume its slow crawl. And we all move on with it, because after all, what other choice do we have?

It's been a week since Colm's funeral, and today we will open the doors again for the first time, just for a few hours, to get our heads around what has happened and ease ourselves back in gently after the shock. Tomorrow night is going to be a biggie, as a new up-and-coming British singer is booked in. People have been going crazy for her since Danny booked her nearly a month ago, and we're sold out. We can't let them all down and we can't stay closed forever. And I'm confident it's what Colm would have wanted too: to keep Rosie's alive and kicking.

It's just after midday and Christy sits up at the bar with a battered red folder in front of him. 'I'll need a double before I even start this.'

Uh oh. This does not bode well.

I pour a large whiskey and pull up a chair beside him. Danny stays behind the counter and makes us a pot of tea. Christy slugs a good throatful of whiskey, then winces and shakes his head at the teapot. 'You're not going to like this. I suggest you sort yourselves out with something a lot stronger than tea bags for what's coming.'

'Just hit us with it; whatever it is, we can take it,' I tell him. Danny winks at me and pours our tea.

'On second thoughts…' He turns on his heel and grabs two chocolate bars. 'Here you go, just in case.'

'Right. Don't say I never warned you.' Christy opens the folder and flips through to a piece of paper covered in columns and small numbers. And lots of red pen marks, murderous-looking circles and slashes all over the sheet.

He separates it from the rest and holds it in front of him as though he is a town crier. 'Rosie Munroe inherited this pub from her mother and her mother before her. A long line of successful businesswomen. And in their day it was tough going. Rosie never had her own children, so she left the pub to Colm as he was her only living relative, her nephew. I've been Colm's best friend all my life – he was as close as any brother to me. And well, I've seen this place have its good days and its bad days. Sadly, Colm let bad days become bad months and bad years. During one particularly bad year, he found himself in a situation where he had to borrow a lot of money just to keep the show on the road. It seemed sensible at the time.' He cocks an eyebrow. 'You follow me?'

We both nod.

'Well, sensible may be the wrong word. I knew he'd borrowed money from all sorts of lowlife, but I thought I knew the extent of it and that he was keeping on top of it.'

He lowers the paper and peers over it, shaking his head. 'How far from the truth that has turned out to be.'

I'm afraid of what I'm going to hear next.

'As you know, on top of all his loans, Colm also mortgaged and remortgaged to the hilt. Which brings us to the major problem concerning the two of you…'

I lean in to Danny for physical support; by the look on Christy's face, this is serious.

He flicks through to another piece of paper; this one is heavier, embossed with a silver and green logo.

'As Colm owes the bank, and has failed to meet payments over a sustained period of time – and now that he is deceased will never be in a position to repay his debts – the bank have authorised the repossession of this building.' He drains the whiskey.

'But we are the leaseholders,' I tell him. 'And we're turning a profit. They need to speak to us and sort out what kind of repayment programme we can draw up. It's fine, Christy, we can sort it.'

Christy shakes his head and leans forward on his elbows.

'I'm sorry, Evelyn, you only have the lease for the licence.' He pats his hand down on the counter. 'For the bar business, not the premises. The bank own the building and I'm afraid they are turfing you out. As of tomorrow, Rosie Munroe's is closed, under repossession order, and will be registered for public auction as a going concern.'

It's Danny who's now shaking his head. 'No offence, Christy, but that can't be right. Surely the bank want to sort something out…'

Christy takes off his glasses and slumps back in his chair.

'Sure they've been trying to sort things out with Colm for years. He was on his last chance when you guys stepped in to take over.' He wipes his hand down his chin. 'I know you two have worked your bollocks off. And you know, I was just starting to believe that you'd make it. That you were going to save this old girl from extinction.'

Danny has the bank's letter in his hand now, his finger trailing down the page. '"… licence is suspended… notice to stop trading with immediate effect… any attempt to counter these instructions will result in prosecution… trespassing… the premises must be vacant for insurance purposes".' He looks up. 'But what about all the bands we've booked in? What about the stock? The staff? What are they supposed do? Just show up tomorrow and find a sign on the door saying that we're shut? For good. Just like that?' He sounds as outraged and gutted as I feel. Are we really hearing this properly? We have already pre-sold hundreds of tickets online for upcoming gigs!

Christy holds up his hands in defeat.

'What about all the money I've ploughed into this place?' I ask. I know the answer. *Nothing.* I chose to invest in the building, and the building belongs to the bank, so I've got no rights whatsoever.

God, I feel stupid. I thought it was much more clear-cut. It never crossed my mind that the business and the building were two separate entities. It's like when you order an Indian and you just get a bowl of curry, and you realise, at the most inopportune time, that rice and veg and bread and all the other stuff you assumed would come with it doesn't. It's a perfect analogy, exactly the same thing, if your Indian meal cost you thousands and thousands, every last cent of your savings…

I can hear Mrs O'Driscoll's voice in my ear. *To assume makes an ass out of u and me.* So that's where I went wrong. Assuming that I could trust the documentation, assuming that I was given the whole story, assuming that I could make a go of this place and actually succeed.

I sling two shots of whiskey into each of three glasses. Why not? We've lost. We've lost the whole shebang.

'It's the end of the road, I'm afraid,' says Christy, closing the folder.

'But there has to be some way!' says Danny. 'What about the auction? Can anyone bid in that?'

'Oh yes, it's a public auction, so there's nothing to stop you bidding like everybody else. Open house.'

Okay. Maybe there is some way then. An expensive, high-risk, unlikely and unpredictable way, but a way nonetheless. I've watched *Bargain Hunt* enough times to know how to raise my paddle with a haughty nod.

'And how much do you think they'll want for it?'

Christy curls the end of his beard around his finger as he makes the calculations. 'There'll be a reserve on it so that the bank are guaranteed to recoup what they are owed.' He refers back to the paper with the red scribbles. 'According to this – and I'm no expert – a quarter of a million might cover it. Absolute minimum, though. Remember, the bank is not there to chase the best price or make a profit; they just want to reclaim the debt and strike it off their books. Some clever fox with a healthy savings account could snap up a real bargain here.'

'Two hundred and fifty thousand euros.' I blow out my cheeks. 'I know it's a great price for a place like this, but it's still a small fortune. I have nowhere near that.' I look to Danny.

He tilts his head, considering. 'I think I could raise about twenty thousand if I sell off all the recording equipment Rory had; it's in storage.'

And that prompts me. 'If I could sell the cottage, I'd have a lump sum that might give us a fighting chance. But not the whole amount, that's for sure. And we don't have a buyer yet.' I haven't had a sniff of interest, even at the reduced-to-sell price tag. And until I sell it, I'm tied to my previous life. It could be months, years even, before a buyer comes along – and with nobody in it, damp creeping in, no regular maintenance, it's depreciating all the time. Who knows if we'll ever sell it at all, never mind at a decent price.

Christy shakes his head. 'I don't want to dash your dreams, kids, but that's only a drop in the ocean. These banks don't wait around; they want the cash fast and they don't care where they get it from.' He looks around the bar, waves his arms. 'Place like this is a developer's dream. They'll be licking their lips when they see it on the market. Location, period features, iconic, blah blah blah. Mark my words, the next time you see it, it will be boarded up and gutted and sliced up into office space, filled with water coolers and photocopiers and soul-crushed sales staff before you can blink.'

I think about Martin, the homeless man I met when I'd just arrived here in Dublin, living – barely surviving – on the developer's steps.

I glance over at Danny. He's deep in thought too. If this was a church or a theatre, we'd get a preservation fund, we'd be able to prove it was a site of cultural heritage. But we've just got some bar-stool anecdotes to prove its place in history. And that won't stand. Every pub in Dublin would declare that they inspired the greats if it was easy as that. But it's not just about the history, it's about the present, too. We've got new bands banging down the door to play on our stage, to our crowd. It's not fair. It's worse than that; it feels unjust.

Danny wraps his arm around my shoulder. 'We'll find another place. If we can do it here, we can do it again.'

It's as if he's read my mind. It *is* about the future. When I think of my five-year plan now, it's all about Rosie Munroe's. The music, the staff, the direction, the advertising. It's about me and Danny building it into our shared dream as partners. Making that dream a reality. A little space carved out away from the sirens and the fumes; somewhere people can go just to escape the drudgery, the pressures of life, the loneliness for a short while.

I just know that if we could raise enough to buy this place, we'd bring it even further. We could make it happen. Look what we have done already. We've quadrupled the profits, and that's considering all our setting-up expenses, bar stock and initial promotion costs. We've just got our name on the map, we're just starting to go places, make a solid reputation for ourselves, reach the dizzying heights we've worked so hard for.

Don't say it's all over, that it's all been for nothing, that our dream is done. Don't say Rosie Munroe's has died along with Colm.

Christy rings the bell, a sad, drawn look in his eyes. 'Last orders, ladies and gents, looks like it's time to go.'

Looks like it's our time to say goodbye.

CHAPTER TWENTY-FIVE

We've cancelled everything. Made our devastating announcements over social media, tried to explain that it was unforeseen, unexpected, that whatever gut-wrenching disappointment the punters are feeling, believe us, we are feeling it too. Yesterday a huge red 'For Public Auction' sign was erected out front. Every window is boarded up with chipboard so it's pretty clear it is a vacated property, but there's still lots of stuff to steal if somebody was that way inclined; everything from the memorabilia to the fittings, from the floorboards to the stained-glass windows.

It depresses me so much to see it this way. Only a couple of weeks ago we were riding the crest of a wave, we had everything to dream about; now it's just a boarded-up building that amounts to nothing more than the numbers in red on a banker's ledger. Cancelling stock orders, cancelling gigs we'd booked in, breaking the news to the staff that the doors would never reopen, handing over the keys to the auctioneer and switching off the lights for the last time was heartbreaking.

Danny took his guitar back out to the corner of the street and started busking again, but facing the tomb of Rosie Munroe's hurt him too much, so he moved into the centre of town, where there's still plenty of life. He sings on the Ha'penny Bridge now.

He's been quiet lately. Quieter than I've known him to be since we've been together.

This morning, in the very early hours, he's restless in his sleep, tossing and turning and groaning. Then all of a sudden, he shoots up with a jolt.

'Are you okay, Danny?' I ask, turning on the bedside lamp and putting my hand on his shoulder.

He looks at me, clutches his chest and then his cheeks.

'I dreamt it happened to me,' he says, his eyes big and unblinking. 'The heart attack.'

'What do you mean?' I ask, gathering the bedclothes. Whatever this is, it has scared the crap out of Danny, and that's scared the crap out of me.

'Rory died of a congenital heart defect.'

Ah. I always wondered how Rory had died, but couldn't bring myself to ask. I didn't want to ask questions that may deepen Danny's grief even more.

'We never knew he had it until the day his heart just stopped. He was my twin, so the doctors told me it was fairly reasonable to assume that if it was hereditary, I might have it too.'

'You?' I can barely get my words out. No. No. This can't be right. I shake my head and turn towards him. 'But they'd be able to tell you, right? They wouldn't keep you in the dark about that if you were at risk. There's got to be some kind of test, so you don't have to go through your life not knowing. Not knowing would be hell, torture.'

He shakes his head. 'They've offered me tests; they can tell me easily if I'm at risk, but I don't want to know.'

'I don't get this, Danny. Help me understand why you wouldn't want to know something as important, as literally life-changing as this?'

'Because that's exactly it. If they tell me I've got it, that changes my life. Ruins my life. Imagine they told me that I only had a year to live, what would that do to my present? Totally fuck it up. I'd just spend the year worrying and waiting. I don't want that to happen to me. That's not living. That's hell. That's torture.'

I sit up fully in bed now and turn on the light.

'But what if they told you that you were fine, that you have the heart of an ox? Then you'd really be able to live fully, without fear…'

He shrugs. 'It's a risk I'm willing to take.'

'So you're never going to find out? How do you plan ahead? How do you think about what you'll be doing in five years' time?'

He shakes his head resolutely. 'I never look ahead. I just live for the moment.'

'What if you were with somebody who actually loved you and cared about you? What about the future then, and all the plans you'd have together? What if you had kids?'

'Kids? In a perfect world, yes, kids would be amazing, but that's not going to happen. I'm never going to have any.' He bites down on his bottom lip and stares straight ahead at the bedroom wall. 'My parents didn't exactly do a great job, and our tickers don't seem to be the strongest, so I figure it's probably best for the human race that I don't put another generation through all that.'

I need to know the answer to this next question even if it has the potential to make my whole world implode. Again.

'Where *do* you see yourself in five years' time, Danny?'

He shrugs. 'No idea.'

And I have no idea what else to say. We sit in silence, trying our best not to look at each other now. Danny pulls on a T-shirt and shorts and heads into the bathroom.

Once he is in the shower, I slink out of the front door. I should want to kick myself for asking the five-year question. But the problem doesn't lie in the question. The problem lies with the answer. And the answers I've had have been the kiss of death for both the men I thought I could build a forever with.

CHAPTER TWENTY-SIX

When I get back to Tara's flat, I lie on the single bed and try to work out what I should do next. The hard truth is that it's over for me here. I can't stay on like this. Circling around what will never be, anxiously rubbing at my fading hopes like a rabbit's foot.

Instead of starting over, I've opened old wounds, made things even worse than they were when I arrived here in the first place. I loved my father and then had to bury him, and now I've had to do the same with Colm. I loved the cottage and let myself believe that it would be the place where new memories would be born, new dreams realised, and then I had to empty it out and lock it up just like I've had to do all over again with Rosie's. Worst of all, I believed I could still trust my heart and have a second shot at love and laughter and happy ever after.

Realising I don't have a future with Danny hurts much more than anything else, because it has come as a complete shock. And there is something he could do about it, if only he could pluck up the courage to take the next step in finding out what the truth is.

And of course, it hurts because I'm in love with him. I must be to feel like this.

I'm finished now. I'm heartbroken and exhausted and everything I've worked for since getting here feels so cold, so distant. The same words just go round and round in my head.

What a terrible shame. What a terrible waste. What a terrible end to a so-called brand-new start. I tried. I failed. I think it's time to cut my losses, pack my bags and make my way home to Ballybeg.

The next day I arrange to meet Danny in town for lunch. I think it's for the best. I tried in this city, I threw everything at it, but I guess Colm was right: you just can't beat the system. If anything, I'm worse off than when I first got here, as I managed to sink all my money into Rosie Munroe's and have been left penniless and heartbroken and flat on my arse. When I arrived in Dublin, I couldn't understand how someone like Martin could end up on the street, but now I know exactly how that can happen. Back payments piling up, an interest-rate hike, a few unseen expenses and the next thing you know, you're signing the rights over to the bank and handing in your keys. And if it wasn't for my family, I could easily find myself alone and without a home to go to.

I'm not going to say all this to Danny, obviously. I'm just going to tell him that I'm moving home for a few weeks; to spend some time with my mum and figure out why there is such a big hold-up with the cottage sale. In this market, I don't even know if we'll get as much as we paid for it in the first place. So that can be another debt to add to my accumulating losses. And then there's my divorce. I thought we'd be signed off ages ago, but the last bit of paperwork has yet to come through. At the moment, I just need some space, some time to regroup. I don't have any money left, and moping around Tara's is only making me feel more of a failure.

There are a thousand reasons for me to go home now, and only one to stay. Ruby has hit her stride, and now that she's found her motivation she doesn't really need me anymore. Her confidence has blossomed, through the success of the campaign she ran for us and all the new friends she's made along the way. She's set her sights on this art course she's found and she spends every moment of her spare time adding to her portfolio. Ruby is a girl on a mission and even Moira knows better now than to stand in her way. So there's only Danny. But I can't stay here just for Danny. Especially when our future seems even more precarious than our present. And that's saying something. I've been here before, building my whole life around one person, and to be perfectly honest, I'm too scared to do that again. Because I know it doesn't work. I wish I could say that love is enough, but I know from my own experience that it's not. Love battered by competing dreams and disappointments will only lead me to the same place I've just escaped from.

So with a trembling hand on a heavy heart, I'm here to tell Danny that I'm going home. That he's free to pursue his next adventure without me, without Rosie's and the shackles of our glorious failure. We tried. We failed. We'll survive. Today I'm going to say goodbye and wish him well with a new start, a new beginning for both of us.

I see him on the other side of the street, waiting on the kerb so that he can cross. His phone is hooked into his neck and he is laughing and nodding as he weaves in and out of the stalled traffic. My throat tightens with tears. God, I'm going to miss him. Why did this have to happen to us? We were so close. He's perfect for me, in every way except the way I need. The way that offers us a future together.

If he had the tests and found that he was at risk, that would be our future. I would stand by him all the way. We'd do it together. But to not find out? To just wake up every morning not knowing? Hoping that today isn't the day that you fall to the floor clutching your chest?

I can't do that. I can't bear to.

I pinch the bridge of my nose to stem the tears. I try to shake the emotion from my mind. Rationally, I have no reason to be in Dublin any more. Rationally, I have a warm, comfortable bed waiting for me back in Ballybeg. I may even have a respectable and pensionable job at the school to return to if I make the right noises and pucker up to kiss O'Driscoll's arse appropriately.

Danny spots me across the traffic and waves.

I raise my hand to wave back. It looks like I'm saying hello, but I know it's goodbye.

All those months ago, when I first stepped into the marriage counsellor's office, I believed that I was experiencing what it felt like to be racked with failure, to be heartbroken.

God, I was wrong. So damn wrong.

This is what real failure feels like. *This* is heartbreak.

I stand and smile with my arms now outstretched towards him. I've got be strong for both of us. I'm not going to break. I've packed my bag, I've made my decision, I'm going to deliver this message and get on the last train home today no matter what.

Danny's future is too precious; my future is too precious to waste any more time chasing impossible dreams.

'Hey, so good to see you.' He wraps his arms around me and kisses me on the forehead.

I breathe him in. This isn't going to be easy. Then he spots my bag.

'Where are you off to?' he asks. He probably thinks I'm on a quick visit home to see my mum.

'Let's go and sit down somewhere quiet where we can chat,' I say as he takes the suitcase from me.

Hand in hand, we walk to a nearby café. We order our coffees and sit in the front window, in full view of the passing public outside. He takes both my hands in his across the table. The great big grin hasn't left his face since I met him at the bridge.

'What's up?' I ask. 'You're suspiciously smiley.'

He takes a deep breath. 'I've got some news, Evelyn. Big news. Big good news. I wanted to tell you first, see what you think.'

'Right…' I thought I was the one with news. Big bad news.

'Supanova have asked me to be their guitarist. They want me as part of the band! Remember that agent that gave us his card on opening night. He brought the whole thing together. I showed him the rest of the stuff I've been writing, and he likes it. He says I'm the perfect fit. I can't believe it.' His eyes are wide, and he squeezes my clasped hands in his. 'And that's not all. They want to release the song I sang at Rosie's and for me to co-write the material for the next album, and all being well, the album after that – and who knows? Superstardom!'

I lean across the table and kiss him full on the lips. I know I shouldn't, that it's only going to make things harder, but I can't help it. At least something good has come of all this, and Danny has been recognised for the proper talent he is, as a musician and a songwriter. It's given him his direction back; it's given him an identity. No longer a lone Musketeer singing on the corner without any dream beyond getting through the day.

'Danny, that is wonderful, WONDERFUL news!' I mean every word. This is exactly what he's always dreamed of: performing again, being part of something bigger, making music, being heard, being appreciated. 'I'm so proud of you. Don't forget all about us little guys when you hit the big time.'

He arches his eyebrow. 'Forget? Evelyn, are you mad? I want you with me. I want to do this with you. Say you'll come with me, we'll do it together.'

'Come with you? How on earth can I come with you?'

'Well, now that Rosie's is closed, you're freed up. It might be a bit tough at first, but soon we'll have the royalties coming in and then maybe we can work something out.'

I shake my head. This can't work. I can't follow the band from gig to gig like a spare wheel. Different city every night, rehearsals and after-parties, me hanging around but without a role or purpose beyond being Danny's cling-on girlfriend. That's not me. And it's not what I want for myself, to be his tag-along.

This is a time for Danny to try to make his name as the newest band member; he needs to give that everything. Not try to tend to me and our lives at the same time. It'll never work. And although I really love his optimism, I know from my divorce that stronger relationships than ours have crumbled under this sort of pressure. Add a possible heart problem into the mix, and our future together becomes even more impossible.

'Danny, I can't. This is your dream and I want you to go for it full pelt. This is something you need to do by yourself.'

He takes his hands out of mine, slumps back in his chair and runs his fingers through his hair. 'I'm not hearing this. This doesn't add up. Evelyn, we *know* we want to be together, we *know* we can make this work. Look at the great job you did with Ruby; you could do more private tutoring. Or maybe even pick up some music teaching. Online tutoring. I'm not sure yet, but I know you'll come up with something; you always do.'

He dips his gaze to try to meet my eyes. 'I know it sounds like a big change, and if Rosie's was still open, I'd stay with you there forever, I promise you that. I loved it just as much as you did and we were a team, a cracking team, you and me. But it's gone now, and we can't bring it back.'

I snap my hands away from the table.

'Yes, Danny, I'm fully aware that it's gone. And that's why I wanted to tell you that I'm leaving. I'm going home.'

'For how long?'

'I don't know yet. Maybe for good.'

Now he's shaking his head, baffled, and staring out the window. He looks at me sideways, opens his mouth to speak, but then turns to the window again, like he's trying to process what I'm saying without any success.

'There's nothing here for me any more,' I tell him, trying to swallow back the bubbling emotion from my voice.

'Oh thanks a lot. I thought I actually meant something to you, Evelyn. I didn't realise I was just a business partner with benefits.'

'Don't say that! Don't you dare say that. You are more than that and you know it! But things can't work this way. We both need to share the same vision; you can't sustain working for another person's dream. I don't want to hold you back. You've got your dream, and you need to pursue it. Believe me, I know how this ends. You may think you can live with giving up what you really want, but trust me, as noble and generous as it sounds, it doesn't work. It comes back to bite you – hard. I've been there and done that and I've not come all this way to do it to you. We need to call time on us.'

'No. You're wrong. You are so, so wrong, Evelyn.'

I need to swallow hard. There's so much I want to say to him about my feelings for him, but none of that is going to bring me any closer to getting on that train.

'Danny, I can't commit to someone who can't commit to me.'

'What are you talking about? I'm asking you to be with me! Isn't that commitment? What do you want me to do, ask you to marry you? Is *that* commitment?'

'No!' I snap back. 'That's not it. How can I stay with you and love you and follow you around the world knowing that I could lose you at any time? How can you ask me to hand my future over to you without any certainty that you will even be around to share it with me? I thought we both wanted the forever family, Danny. It's what I want more than anything. And I can't let my chance slip away. You've told me you don't want kids, but I do. There's no real compromise there.'

He looks at me, stunned, then nods slowly. Neither of us is in the wrong. But we're definitely coming at things from opposite sides.

'And what if I get the test and they tell me, yep, I have an identical problem to Rory?'

'Then we'd work through it. We'd find a way. Forewarned is forearmed. We'd get through it. Together.'

'I'm sorry, Evelyn, but I can't do that.'

I nod my head. 'I'm sorry too.'

He opens his mouth again, ready to fight me, ready to try and convince me. 'I'll do anything. I want you. I want us to be together. There's so much ahead of us, if you'll just listen and give us a chance.'

'I've loved being with you, Danny.' The tears are gathering in my throat. 'But I need someone I can build a future with, someone to make plans with, someone who wants a home and a family just as much as I do. I need someone who is looking beyond tomorrow. I understand your reasons. I know why you don't want to do that. And that's why we need to let each other go.'

I stand up and put my coat on.

'This can't be happening. This is a mistake. A huge, huge mistake.' He bites down on his thumb and squeezes his eyes shut.

'Goodbye, Danny.'

I pick up my suitcase, trying not to breathe, not to falter, willing myself not to cry until I'm on the train and safely alone, far enough down the track that I can't turn around and change my mind.

CHAPTER TWENTY-SEVEN

Hours later, I step down from the train in Ballybeg. I've tried texting and calling Mum countless times to tell her I'm on my way home with all my stuff and that I'll need a lift. But there's been no answer, which is completely unlike her.

I sit on the bench at the front of the station and hope that a taxi might pull up, or at least someone I know who can give me a lift. I pick up the local newspaper as I wait and flick through; most of it is made up of births, marriages and deaths, and I know people in every section. I see a huge photo of my ex-colleague Fionnuala in her wedding dress – all by herself. She's so bridezilla, she cut out the groom. I laugh to myself. Nothing changes, until everything does.

I look up at the clock. It's 7 p.m., so there are no more trains in or out for the rest of the evening. I haul my suitcase by the strap and make my way along the potholed road towards town. There's no way I'm going to get home like this – with this bag or in these shoes. I'm hungry. And I'm tired. And I must be run down or getting my period, because my back hurts, my nipples sting and I just feel like I want to sob my heart out. All the time.

I walk to the junction at the top of the road. It is getting dark now, so I decide to continue straight into town, where at least I can call a cab from the pub and rest up for a bit.

I pass the church just as the congregation starts to trickle out. A hand shoots in the air and I hear my name called. It's my mother's hairdresser, Esther.

'How are you, Evelyn! Aren't you looking mighty? Down from Dublin, is it? Very good, very good. And tell me, how is your mother getting on in Rome? She promised to bring me back some holy water. She's a great woman, your mother, I know she'll not let me down.'

Rome… ROME! Of course, Mum has gone to visit the Pope! SHIT!

I thank Esther for her good wishes and wonder what to do next. I can't believe I forgot about her trip, but I've been so busy refurbishing the pub – and then closing down the pub – that I've lost track of what's happening at home. I can't believe that the day I decide to move back, she's not even here. I suppose I could stay in the guest house in town. At least that's close by, and I could have a big dinner and a soak in the bath before crawling under the covers. But that would get back to her and she'd be annoyed. It might even spark a rumour that we'd fallen out, or worse still, that she'd sloped off to Rome without care or consideration for her daughters. That's the kind of thing that would get my mother's knickers in a twist.

Great. What now?

'Evelyn?'

I turn almost as a reflex. At first I don't recognise him. After all, the last time I saw him we were barely on speaking terms and trying to process that our relationship was truly, legally over. Granted, I've seen a few sneaky pics on Facebook, but I didn't expect a transformation this radical.

James is wearing a crisp white shirt with fitted dark jeans. His hair is neatly trimmed, and he's clean-shaven. And tanned. And healthy and toned and bright-eyed.

'Wow,' I say. 'You look great.'

We do an awkward dance where we move towards each other for a kiss on the cheek, but then I pull away, and he pulls away, and we both search the other's face with a mixture of fascination and disbelief.

'You're not looking too bad yourself.'

He offers up that half-smile I know so well, the smile that probably made me agree to date him in the first place. For an instant I am seventeen years old again and the world has stopped because the boy I assumed was out of my league is standing in front of me, speaking to me, looking into my eyes.

I look away. *Don't go there*, I tell myself. What's past is past. James and I had our chance a lifetime ago.

'What happened?' I ask, noticing the cast on his arm. It seems crazy that I didn't know he'd hurt himself. Somehow I've been so wrapped up in the changes in my own life that it's easy to imagine he has just stood still, frozen in time. But I can see that he's changed as a result of our split almost as much as I feel I have.

'Nothing, just a motorcycle accident.'

'Oh James!' It's on the tip of my tongue to tell him off. To tell him that bikes are not safe, that he could kill himself, all the old lines flooding back into my mind, all the warnings I spoke a hundred times when I was his wife. When taking care of him was my job.

He bends down and picks up my suitcase.

'I've got the car here, let me take this for you. Can I give you a lift home?'

'Thanks, James, perfect timing.'

'We can swing by the cottage if you like. I've done a bit of work on it – at long last, right?'

The cottage, of course. Lying empty as though waiting for me to pick up my life where I left off.

James holds the door open for me as I step into the cottage he once carried me into after our wedding. I walk over to the little window and pull back the dainty lace curtains I hung with such pride, such optimism, the day we moved in. The views of the sea are stunning, the position perfect. I fell in love with the place then, and to be honest, I'm still in love with it. To wake up each morning to a vast view of sea and sky is a gift. I often imagined our children traipsing up and down the wooden steps to the beach, wrapped in towels, with tousled sea-salt waves in their hair.

I wince. All those dreams have disappeared with the tide, never to return; the punch of disappointment still hollows my stomach. We could have had it all, James and I – we came so close. Above me, the sky is full of deep grey clouds, rolling east in the wind, and I stand here now on the other side of those dreams. I've learnt to let them go, to accept what's gone and to embrace what is. Real life doesn't co-operate with dreams, with fantasies. No matter how much you want them or what sacrifices you make.

The beach below is empty, and I watch the glowing halo circling the lighthouse. Somewhere in the distance, a dog barks a warning to a real or imagined intruder.

'How's Dublin treating you?' James calls out to me from the kitchen.

I'm not quite sure what to tell him at first. Busy, interesting, different, life-changing… I don't want to get into what happened with Rosie Munroe's. He'll not understand and I will sound silly, like I had no clue about business or contracts or taking on a massive financial risk. And I don't want to talk about Danny, of course. I'll sound silly again, on the rebound, naive, taking on a massive emotional risk. So I just tell him that it's been good, a nice change.

'How was Ibiza?' I ask in return. He shrugs and I notice his face darken but decide not to push him on it. Maybe it's his accident. If his arm is in a cast, it must have been serious. Or maybe there's more. Perhaps something else happened out there. I can't put my finger on it but there is a change in him. Something about his posture, the deep tone of his voice, makes him seem more serious, more intense.

For the most part, our conversation touches only on the surface of things, and for the time being neither of us seems ready to go deeper than that.

'The place looks excellent, James. I love the colour of the walls, and the paintwork. All the holes and patches and cables seem to have disappeared!'

He shrugs. 'I should have done it a long time ago.'

He lights the fire and we sit in our old chairs, cradling our glasses of wine and listening to the crashing waves outside. The wind whistles through the gaps in the windows and doors and I notice that the clouds have balled together the way they do when it's getting ready to storm. The first blinks of lightning begin to register on the distant horizon, making the world outside flash as if someone were taking photographs of us, capturing this crazy snapshot of two exes sitting together like the perfect couple in the most idyllic setting when the truth is so far from how it might appear. How is it that we can sit like this, be this comfortable together now, when we couldn't when we were still married?

In the moonlight, his face is half in shadow. 'Evelyn. We need to talk.'

'I know. We haven't had a single offer on the cottage all this time. The work you've done is excellent, James. Hopefully it might attract some interest now.'

It takes a moment for him to answer me, his words floating in the firelit darkness.

'Not about the cottage,' he whispers. 'About us. About me and you.'

I look up at him, trying to read his face. What does he mean? There is no *us* any more.

He swirls his wine before looking at me. 'I should have listened to you. You were right and I was... I was an ass.'

A log sparks, sending trails of smoke up the chimney. He adds more wine to our glasses. I reach my hand over the rim of my glass to stop his overly generous pour.

'I've been picturing this for months. What I'd say when I saw you. *If* I ever saw you. And I promised myself that if I did get the chance to speak to you again, if you'd give me the time, I'd tell you exactly how I feel. No holding back, because what I've realised is that I have nothing left to lose.'

His eyes drift to the window. He stands and slowly walks the length of the living room and back. He's thinking, so I give him a moment.

'I fucked it up, Evelyn. And I'm sorry.'

I look away from him momentarily, not wanting see the struggle in his eyes.

'Are you okay, James? Did something happen to you in Ibiza?'

He nods. 'For the first couple of weeks I thought I was living the dream. Everything was how I'd imagined it would be: paradise. I partied all night, slept all day, ate well, drank well. I took full advantage of my freedom, let's say.' He glances over at me, shame and sadness in his eyes.

'James, you don't have to apologise to me. You're a single guy. You are free to do as you please. This is what we wanted, both of us. I wanted you to have your freedom, so I'm glad you made the most of it.'

He shakes his head. 'That's the problem. I couldn't handle the freedom. I spun out of control.'

I nod towards his arm. 'Is that how that happened?'

He rubs his chin and laughs drily. 'If only this was all of it. I spun out of control in every way. And by the second month, things had started to go tits up. I was waking up with no idea where I'd been. Do you know where I was on the morning of my birthday? I woke up on a pillow covered in animal-print fake fur on the floor of a bedroom I didn't recognise with a woman I couldn't remember even speaking to. And I thought, what the hell am I doing? I don't want to be here. I want to be at the cottage. I want to turn over in my beautiful bed and kiss my beautiful wife and know that I've got everything I need. And that's when it dawned on me. I had everything I needed and I let it slip away.'

There are traces of tears in his eyes. I have never seen James cry... never.

'I tried to remember how I'd got there: a vague image of a bar and then a club after that. Neon strobe lighting, neon drinks, everything after that a complete black hole.'

'James, it's fine. It's just a drunken one-night stand. People have them. It's no big deal. Not worth beating yourself up about.' I feel like this is cathartic for him. Like he needs to tell me everything now that he's built himself up to do so. I don't know where it's going but the least I can do is listen. Poor James, whatever went wrong, it's had a profound effect on him.

'There's more. There's so much more I need to tell you.' It sounds like he's pleading with me. What can I do but stay and hear him out? We were together a long time. And even though I'm not sitting here as his wife or his lover, I can be here as his friend. I owe him that.

'It wasn't just a one-night thing, Evelyn. I'd been doing it for months. Night after night after night, relentlessly. I looked at myself in the mirror and told myself to get a grip. That I wasn't having fun any more. I got it all wrong. I thought I'd feel light and carefree and as though I was living for the moment, but I didn't. I felt heavy and pained and lonely.'

'Is that why you came back?' I ask.

He shakes his head. 'No. I thought it would pass. I thought I just needed time to get my head around everything. Figure out what had happened. And what had happened? I was happy, then I wasn't. I was married, then I wasn't. I was here, then I was there. Well, none of that really explains how two people who thought they'd spend the rest of their lives together wake up one day and realise that they hardly know the person lying next to them.'

I simply nod, when really all I want to do is tell him how hearing him out is the last thing my heart can take right now. I can't bear that he was in so much pain all by himself.

'You did the right thing by coming home. By taking care of yourself.'

He fidgets with his watch strap and then pinches the bridge of his nose. I'm a complete wreck as I sit here and wait.

'One day, I tore off on my motorbike. Thinking I need to break this cycle, get out of the strip of bars and clubs. I needed some space. Some nature, some quiet, somewhere with no neon lights or happy hours. But all the time in my head, I was thinking how stupid I'd been. How momentously I'd screwed up. It felt good to ride out into the wild, to follow the road as it got greener and more lush. I was too far out from any shelter when a storm started to rumble in the distance, and then the rain lashed down. It was dark, and the road was slippery, so I missed the bend in the road and my back wheels started to spin. I panicked. Next thing there was a huge crashing sound and I came off the bike.'

I've covered my eyes, my image of James injured on the side of the road too clear in my mind.

'When I came around, the rain had stopped, but I was covered in shattered glass, and my arm was crumpled at the wrong angle. The pain was worse than anything I'd ever felt before.'

I lean my elbow into the couch and cover my mouth with my trembling hand.

'And that's when I thought, this is it. I'm going to die. And right after that, I had a second realisation that stung more than anything else: no one would miss me. I looked up at the stars, and I thought of you, Evelyn, trying to teach me the constellations on the first night we moved into our little cottage. And how I didn't listen. I never listened. I have been an unbelievable arsehole. A lazy, ungrateful, selfish git.'

He is sobbing now, just letting the tears run down his cheeks. I slide in beside him and put my arm around his shoulders.

'It's okay, James, you're here now. Everything is okay.'

He nods his head and blinks back the tears. 'I kept searching the sky and I swore to myself that if I survived this, I would change, I would be the man I promised you I'd be the night I proposed all those years ago. Because I get it now. You know what love is, Evelyn, you know how it should feel – that's why you called time on us. And you were right. And that just makes me love you and admire you even more.'

I close my eyes and soak up his words. I never knew this, never imagined it. When we went our separate ways, I always assumed James was having a fantastic time, living exactly as he wanted, partying and being free as a bird. I never expected this. I'm not sure at this point what else to expect. After several quiet moments, I reluctantly open my eyes.

He is on one knee now; he takes my hand in his. My breath catches in my throat. *No, James… Please, please no…*

'Evelyn Anne Dooley, this time things will be different. I want forever with you, here in this cottage. I want the family, I want it all. This time I will be the man you deserve.'

Shaking my head, I slowly withdraw my hand, then sink down on my knees to face him.

'James, you think I am what you want. But I'm not. You don't want to go back; neither of us do. You need to make room for the new stuff; you need to get rid of everything that doesn't make you happy and stop it blocking all the light and the goodness and the adventure that's waiting to get in. You will *always* be my first love, James. But you will have a last love too, and that isn't me. It will be some beautiful girl with dreams as big and bright as yours, and when you are with her, you'll know that you align perfectly and she makes you shine your brightest self. And until you meet her, don't settle, okay? She may be the first person you meet tomorrow, or it may take a bit more time than that, but if you look for her, she will appear. And that's when you'll know you've found your forever, James. Promise me?'

I could say this with utter conviction. I could tell him without flinching with doubt or with uncertainty. Because that was what I had found with Danny.

He nods. I pull him against my chest and together we say goodbye to our past, and make room for everything that's out there for us now that we've learned our lessons about life and love and letting go.

Those lessons have been hard. Cruel and heartbreaking. But one thing is for sure, we've learnt never to make the same mistakes again.

James drops me home, and just before I get out of the car and say goodnight, he tells me not to worry about the cottage; that he'll sort it out. That it's the least he can do for me.

I thank him, and then I wave him goodbye.

CHAPTER TWENTY-EIGHT

'Evelyn! It's me, Mum, I'm home!'

And soon the house is full of sounds: sizzling bacon, the rumble of the washing machine, the whistling kettle and Mum's little transistor radio belting out her favourite country music. Muffin bounds up the hallway and jumps onto my duvet, licking me and sniffing me and wagging her big bushy tail. Yes, I'm back to square one. Again. But other than Muffin's panting halitosis, it's not the worst square on the board.

'I'm in the kitchen, Evelyn! What a lovely surprise to arrive home and find you here. I've the tea on, come down when you're ready.'

I look at the clock on the bedside table. Eleven o'clock! Since James and I made our peace, I've been staying at home waiting for Mum to get back, sleeping like a baby for twelve hours a night.

In many ways, the day I left Dublin was a dark day. It took a lot out of me. Who'd have thought that I'd ever have to say goodbye to Danny? Who'd have thought that I'd have to say goodbye to James again? Poor James. Everything he said that night, about being ready for a family, ready for us, I would have given anything to hear him say a year ago. If that was how he'd felt before, we'd probably have tried harder to work things out, to stay together. We might even have a baby by now. I'd still be a teacher at St Mary's; we would still be at the cottage.

But it's too late to rewind to what might have been. Too much time has passed, too much has happened. If he had uttered those words in the marriage counsellor's office that day, the whole course of our lives could have steered in a different direction. He might never have had his hard-won epiphany in Ibiza and I would never have met Danny. I would never have moved to Dublin or taken on Rosie's or met Ruby or Colm or Christy. So much could have been different if we had stayed the same. But last night made me realise something: that I don't regret any of it. I don't want to rewind and change the steering of the course; I don't want a second chance at a life I wanted to escape the first time around.

Even now, back in this bed, back in my mother's house, I feel like I've been somewhere. I feel like I've lived, I've learned, I've tried something different and new. And as a result, *I* am different and new. And I'm not the only one. I had a lovely long Skype chat with Ruby last night; she's applied for the bursary I told her about that supports higher-education funding for students from disadvantaged backgrounds. I found the number online and then rang up to explain to the administrator exactly how much adversity Ruby has overcome to try and get a place on an art foundation course. I've vouched for her, but ultimately she has to make the case herself, and her work must be good enough to qualify. This is her big opportunity. And only she can make it happen from here. She sounded excited, though, fired up and ready to go, so fingers crossed she channels that energy the right way.

I feel shattered, like I'm in recovery somehow, maybe because I'm rebuilding, transforming, shedding old layers. I ache in every part of my body.

'Tea's made!' Mum yells. A nice big mug of sugary tea, yes, that's what this rebuild needs.

With all the agility of a ninety-year-old, I swing my feet over the side of the bed and stand. I catch a glimpse of myself in the mirror. I look shocking: pale and spotty. Puffy. And hung-over despite the fact that I haven't drunk anything in ages. Lately, the mere thought of drink just hits me in the throat, and the next thing I know I feel close to getting on my knees and arching over the toilet bowl, puking from the pit of my stomach. I seem to enter into some kind of masochistic game of thinking of things that make me want to puke even more… kebab… uggghhh; runny egg… ugghh; ashtrays… UGGHHHH.

I can't let my mum see me looking like this. She'll think the worst. I've come home and I look sick. She'll immediately think that I've developed a heroin addiction.

'Just getting ready! Be there in a minute.'

I step out onto the landing. Even the salty scent of bacon is making me want to gag. Maybe I am actually sick; this isn't normal. I lock the bathroom door. I really don't feel well at all. With my cheek pressed against the cool tiled wall, my right hand finds the hot tap and I start to run the bath. I've always had bad periods, especially during times of stress, so I guess that would explain how I'm feeling now. Between the pub and Colm and Danny and moving back home and then meeting up with James, I guess it's no surprise that…

Wait a minute.

It's been way longer than a month since I've had a period.

I'm usually like clockwork every month. Even when I was in the middle of exams or going on holiday or even on my honeymoon, my period arrived like a pedantic jobsworth. Now *this* is definitely not normal.

I hold my fingers up in front of my face. I really need twenty-eight fingers right now to work this out. I do some rough maths in my head. Then completely disregard it. I take my phone out of my dressing gown pocket and use the calculator. And the calendar. And only then does it actually sink in that – holy shit – I am three weeks late.

Three weeks.

A sharp pain shoots through my breasts and another wave of nausea ripples through me.

Sweet Jesus. It couldn't mean… I can't be…

Just over a month ago, it was opening night at Rosie Munroe's; just over a month ago, I went back to Danny's for the first time.

Oh my God. What if this is what I think it is? What if it's real and it's happening? To me?

Is it possible that I could be properly and legitimately up the duff?

'Evelyn, phone!' my mother calls from the hallway.

I sit on the toilet and rub my hands down my face. I feel tears rising, but weirdly, not tears of sadness; tears of *wow*. Tears of *thank you*. Tears of *how amazing*. Shocking but wow, thank you, amazing…

'Evelyn, it's the solicitor about the cottage. Can you come?'

'No!' I shout, just before my stomach surges into my mouth and I plunge my head into the toilet bowl.

I wake up, startled to hear my mum pounding on the bathroom door. 'Are you okay? Evelyn, answer me! Are you all right in there?'

There is a gross, acidic taste in my mouth and I am draped over the toilet seat. The bath is still running, so I rush over and turn it off just as the water reaches the rim. Unlocking the door, I stand facing her.

'Oh my, Evelyn, you're as white as a sheet. Has something happened?'

I want to say that yes, I definitely think something has happened. I think that something is happening right now. But I don't know for certain. It could be a gastric bug, food poisoning or something stress-related, a result of being run-down. Maybe I've got it wrong. I've missed a period and I'm sick. That's all I've got to go on. There could be other explanations. I'm going to have to find out either way, for certain. And I want to find out right now.

'Any chance we could go into town?' I ask her. 'I need to pick up something at the pharmacy.'

Mum nods, lip pursed, never taking her eyes off me. 'I'll get my keys.'

As I fasten my seat belt in the passenger seat of my mother's car, the impossibility of the task ahead hits me. How on earth am I going to go into the tiny pharmacy in Ballybeg with my mother and secretly buy a pregnancy test?

It cannot be done.

Seriously. This is completely impossible. Because even if I shake her off for ten minutes, even if I could manage to lose her at the butcher's or sneak off when she's in deep conversation with someone from church that she'll inevitably meet, I would have to ensure that the pharmacy is completely empty of people so that word doesn't get back to her from a nosy customer. Or the pharmacist, or whoever is on the till... Actually, the only way I can see myself acquiring a pregnancy test is to shoplift one.

Alternatively, I could just come clean and tell her what's up with me. That would be the most simple and logical way to overcome this. I am a grown woman. This should be easy. I open my mouth. And close it again.

Maybe shoplifting isn't so difficult.

I open my mouth a second time, but before any words come out, my mother's hand in on my knee.

'Whatever it is, you can tell me.'

How does she do that? How do mothers just know?

'Go on, just talk to me, Evelyn. Whatever it is, I'm here for you and you know I will support you with everything I have. So please, stop me worrying and just spit it out.'

I take a deep breath. I want to tell her. I just don't know where to start.

'You can start at the beginning or the middle or the end. I just need to know what's going on with you. I'm your mother and I need to know.'

I still can't seem to find the words. I remember when a school friend of mine got pregnant when we were about eighteen, my mother acted like it was the end of the world, not just because she was young, but because she felt her life was now ruined and that the baby wouldn't have the stability of a family. She sat Tara and me down at the dining room table to receive 'the talk', the beginning, middle and end of which consisted solely of telling us that the only contraception we need concern ourselves with was abstinence.

I look into the wing mirror, trying to decide whether to come clean. I'm not even sure if I am pregnant yet. Yes, I'm divorced and single and jobless and broke, but not so sure about the pregnant bit yet. What a star daughter I turned out to be. Best to wait and check for certain. If I am, I will tell her, no question. And if I'm not, then there is no point in causing unnecessary fuss.

'I'm fine, Mum, just a bit under the weather. A few days' rest and I'll be grand.'

My mother swerves into the side of the road and brakes hard. She turns off the engine and I realise that she's serious. She wants to know. And it looks like neither of us is going anywhere until she gets her way.

'Right, maybe I should go first,' she says. 'I had a lot of time to do some soul-searching when I was in Rome, so here goes.' She places her hand on my knee again and pats it gently, but keeps her eyes fixed on the horizon ahead.

'I only ever wanted you to be happy. When your dad died, I was desperately heartbroken. I wanted to press pause on life. Put everything on standstill, keep everything close and safe. I couldn't cope with reality. When you said you were getting married and were going to stay local, I thought – selfishly – *Thank God. I won't be alone.* And I put my needs, my fears, ahead of your happiness. For that I am deeply ashamed.'

I nod, tears welling in my eyes. I've never heard my mother speak this way, so candidly, so openly. And I've never heard her say she felt ashamed before. Certainly not like this.

She glances off to the side, retreating into the past.

'He was wonderful, your dad – the love of my life. I knew he was the one for me. He listened to me. He always paid attention. There is no greater way to show love than by paying full attention. Inspecting the tiny details of someone else's character like they are precious diamonds, sparkling in between our pinched fingers. Your father made me feel that way from the very first day we spent together. Like every word counted, like every glance was sacred, every moment was a gift, a celebration, an opportunity to love.' She places her other hand on top of mine and strokes it affectionately. 'But you know all this, you loved him too.'

We smile at each other, at his memory, at the memory of the fun we had, all those good times.

'I miss him. And I've been less without him. And I want to say sorry, my darling.' She opens her watery eyes to meet my gaze, spinning her wedding ring around her finger. We both slip back in our seats, resting our heads to the side. I reach out and hold her by the hand, her fingers frail and soft in mine.

'Mum, there's no need.'

'There is, Evelyn. The truth is, I understand why you split from James. I could see you diminishing. And then I was scared that you'd diminish further if you took off somewhere full of strangers, and that would beat you down and hurt you further. What could I do? The parental dilemma – wanting to protect you and toughen you up at the same time; wanting to give you wings but also keep you in the nest with me...'

'It's okay, Mum, *I'm* okay – you don't have to worry about me. I'm all right by myself, I promise.'

'When you become a parent, you have conversations with your kids about what they want to be when they're older. And you press them to say "teacher" or "dentist". But what you really mean is that you want them to make their way in the world so they can be happy. The short answer is I want my children to be happy. Somehow I think I've garbled that message along the way. And it's unintentional, but I realise that I'm in some way to blame for making you unhappy and adding pressure to you. And I want to say that you never have to fear what I will think, because my thoughts will always lead back to you, my wonderful, brave, kind daughter, and the fathomless love I have for you.' She taps her chest. 'All in here. Always here.'

I am a blubbing mess now. She hands me her tissue.

'So forgive me, Evelyn. I was wrong to add to your hurt after you and James broke up. I should have supported you, but I punished you and I can only try to make up for that now. Maybe we have all believed lies about how romance and marriage should be, but I tell you this one thing I've learned: when you are at home alone, all you miss is love. The feeling of it, the memory of it, the ache of its absence.'

She wipes her nose and straightens up. 'So now, if you're ready, tell me. What's going on?'

I *am* ready now. I am ready to talk and I know that she is ready to listen. And together, whatever lies ahead, I know that I will make it, because I have this amazing woman backing me all the way. We have reached a new understanding, and we sit here not as mother and child, but as two women who have loved each other for as long as time itself; we are my forever family.

I start at the beginning. I tell her all about the pub and how amazing it was to build it up, to watch it grow. And then I tell her about Colm dying and Christy breaking the news that we needed to close up, and how the place is up for auction and how overnight we lost everything we'd worked for. I explain that that's where all my savings went, so I'm pretty much on the breadline. And then I tell the part of the story that is new to me. The part that I don't even know yet. The part that may change every story hereafter.

When I've finished, she turns the key and starts the engine.

'And this Danny is a good lad, then?'

'Oh yes, he's a very good lad,' I tell her. 'You'd like him. He took good care of me.'

She gives a sideways glance at my tummy. 'I bet he did.' Brightness flushes her cheeks, and for the first time since we said goodbye to my father, I see my mother's smile flood back into every feature in her face.

We swerve back into the road and the fear lifts from my shoulders. Because whatever happens now, the days of pretending and hiding are long behind me.

CHAPTER TWENTY-NINE

Once we are back home, my mother takes Muffin out for a walk and I have some time to myself. There's just one thing on my mind. Just one job that I need to do. I prepare myself to discover that it might all be in my imagination. That the stress theory could still be the actual reason, in which case I'm going to have to get checked out by my doctor and that might mean change of a completely different kind: a string of tests and blood samples and visits to clinics and medication.

Whatever happens, I need to begin. I take a deep breath, close my eyes and thrust the white plastic stick underneath me. I try to muster the best, longest and straightest stream of wee in the history of squatting women. Bingo, I pee like a racehorse and seem to hit the tiny target according to the instructions: so far so good. Now all I can do is wait.

I sit on the edge of the bath and stare at the wee-soaked stick for exactly one hundred and eighty seconds. Then I raise it to my eyes, fully expecting an answer of some kind. An emoji, a tick or a cross, the pink lines as described on the box…

There is nothing there. It looks the same as it did when I first unwrapped it.

I shake it. I hold it up to the ceiling and then turn it upside down towards the floor.

No change.

I set it down on the side of the sink and wait. Maybe I should do another one. Is it faulty? Or I have I imagined this whole thing and jumped headlong into something without proper evaluation? It's not like this'd be the first time that has happened.

Maybe my dates are wrong. Maybe my phone calculator isn't working. Maybe I had a period in between and forgot. Maybe it was such a light period I didn't even realise it was a period. Maybe I'm just completely losing my mind.

I'm disappointed. This test is a bit like flipping a coin; the result can often help you discover what you really want. But it's not giving me heads or tails; it's a coin that's been flipped and landed on its side, teetering between two completely different outcomes.

The phone rings in the hallway. I'm not in the mood to answer it; I don't want to talk to anyone right now. Mum's out, so I'm sure if they want her they'll ring back or leave a message. If they want me, they can call my mobile.

It stops ringing, and seconds later, I hear my phone ring out from my jacket pocket. It's an unknown number, probably a sales call, but I take it just in case it is an emergency of some sort.

'Hello, Ballybeg Real Estate here, is this Evelyn Dooley?'

'It is.'

'Co-owner of The Cottage, Sea Walk, Ballybeg?'

'That's right.'

'Great, we've been trying to get hold of you. We've had some news regarding the sale of your cottage. I'm happy to inform you that an offer has been made on your property. Cash buyer, no chain. Full amount. They would like to take occupancy immediately.'

I double-check. This sounds too good to be true. Did some millionaire just rock up to Ballybeg sometime this morning with a burning desire to drop everything and move into the cottage? I only saw James last night and he never mentioned a viewing, which he would have done if he'd known about it.

'So someone is buying the cottage for cash without even seeing it first? I'm sorry, but this doesn't add up. I think there has been some kind of mix-up – perhaps you have another cottage on your books?'

I hear the rustle of pages and a cupped hand over the phone whilst some enquiring whispers take place. Sounds like it is a mistake after all.

Two disappointments in one morning. Not sure how much more of this I can take.

'Ms Dooley? Are you still there?'

'Yes, still here,' I answer flatly.

'I've checked our files and consulted with my colleagues, and I can assure you there is no mistake.'

I stand from the rim of the bath and try to process what this means.

It means freedom.

It means I'm no longer tied to James, or the cottage. It means I've got some money in my account. And with all that, I'm back in action. And back in action means moving forward.

'Well, I don't know what to say! That's fantastic! Yes. You'll have to run it by Mr O'Connor, of course, but as far as I'm concerned, that sounds exactly what we wanted, more than we'd hoped for.'

The realtor laughs down the line. 'Well, considering it's Mr O'Connor who has put in the offer himself, I doubt you're going to find him contesting it!'

'I'm sorry, did I hear you correctly? Did you say that the offer came from James?' I'm more confused than ever.

'That's right. He's buying you out so he will be the sole owner. He has added an extra amount as he believes he owes you for interior work that you carried out on the property that has enhanced its value over time.'

Oh James.

'So the amount you will receive, should you accept, will be two hundred and twenty thousand euros. Are you happy for me to proceed?'

Oh. My. God.

'Yes,' I tell him breathlessly. *Two hundred and twenty thousand euros.* 'Please proceed.'

I have no air in my lungs. This is just amazing. Closure for both of us. A chance for James to start afresh in the cottage and enough of a nest egg for me to move out of Mum's house and set myself up with my next step. Whatever the next step is.

'Thank you, Ms Dooley. We'll be in touch if we need anything from you.'

I am so proud of James. It makes sense to me now. He must have held off until he knew for certain that we were not getting back together. If I hadn't come home and met up with him, who knows how long he would have waited? This tells me he's finally accepted it. That he's listened. And understood. And that he's ready for the next step too.

Just as I thank the realtor and hang up, something catches my eye. I pick up the stick and stare at it in disbelief.

Where there was a blank white window, now there are two pink lines.

But... When did...? How...? Wait...

I hold it right up to my face, in front of my nose, and stare at it cross-eyed until I can't focus any longer. Because there they are. There are now undoubtedly TWO very pink lines in the little window at the top of the stick.

I grab the back of the box and reread the instructions. I actually read them out loud so I don't misunderstand. '"Two pink lines indicate a positive pregnancy."' I look from box to stick, box to stick, box to stick. I stand up on the closed toilet seat and push out the little window, holding the stick in the sunshine just to check the lines are still there in the open air, in the natural light. They are not budging; if anything, the line on the right is getting even pinker.

I turn the stick upside down and shake it all about.

Those lines ain't moving. Two pink freakin' lines.

How can it be that my whole life has changed in the space of five minutes, somewhere between the sink and the toilet in this little bathroom?

I feel as though I can hear Colm's rasping voice in my ear. *Master plan, Evelyn, it's all part of the master plan.*

I hear Mum and Muffin crunching the gravel as they walk back up the path. Wait till she gets a load of this!

Two pink lines. I place the positive pregnancy test in my cupped hands and make my way down the hallway, carrying it like it is the most cherished piece of plastic the world has ever seen.

It's the most cherished piece of plastic in my world, that's for sure.

CHAPTER THIRTY

I wait in the kitchen for Mum, wanting to surprise her. But I hear a car stop in front of the house, and she's talking to the driver, whoever it is. It could be anyone from the postman to a lost tourist. Once she gets chatting, she could be a long time, so I stick the kettle on and wait for my news to sink in.

I place my hand on my tummy and try to imagine all that's going on in there. The new human assembly line. The wondrous creation of a brand-new living being, all happening behind my belly button. It's unfathomable. It's overwhelming. I can't believe it's happening, because even though my body appears to be doing the work, my mind had no idea that I was pregnant until I chucked my guts up this morning. Now that I really know it *is* happening, I'm excited and not nearly as scared as I thought I would be.

For starters, I understand that Danny might not be as excited about it as I am. I know his fears; I know he'll be worried. I'd love to imagine that he'd want to be part of this baby's life. I'd love to imagine he'd want to be part of *my* life. I already miss him. I miss everything about him. And I will be able to tell this baby that I love their father very much. Because I do. But even if he's not a father like mine was to me, living in the same house and available all the time, we can still work it out. That's what families do, whatever shape they take. And the fact that he has told me about the potential for heart trouble means that I can let the doctors know straight away. They can monitor, they can advise, they can do all sorts of miraculous things if we start early and get fully on board with what may or may not lie ahead.

This does not faze me. Pregnancy? Birth? Single parenthood? I'm ready for everything.

And then it occurs to me: it's not just about me any more.

With my finger, I trace a heart around my belly button and whisper, '*We* are ready for everything.'

I hear a car door shut outside and the mumble of a low male voice chatting with my mum. It's probably James, wanting to finalise some paperwork or get my signature on a document. I'm glad he feels he can call up here, come in for tea. I'd like to think that now we're on the other side of this, we can be friends.

But when I peek through the curtains, I see that it's not James's car at all; it's a cab. And unmistakably, the tall, smiling man with the dark auburn hair and the chocolate-brown eyes following my mother to the front door is Danny.

My hands fly to my face and I can feel my heart thumping in my chest. What the hell is he doing here? In Ballybeg? With my mother!

There are a thousand things that should be going through my head right now, but the one that elbows out all the others is that he came after me. He's found me. He had his chance to tour, to play, to follow his dream. I let him go, but he's here.

My heart soars in my chest. Danny is here.

I scramble past my mother as she enters the hallway. I swing the front door wide and race down the path. When I reach him, I look into his big dark eyes. He's smiling at me, and for the first time since the moment I met him, we're looking at each other without a trace of fear or reservation.

'You're here. Since when is Ballybeg a stop on the Supanova tour?' I smile.

He shakes his head. 'Too wild for Supanova out here.' He glances over his shoulder: fields to the left, waves to the right. A braying donkey is the only sound in the distance. 'I thought I'd brave it by myself.'

He looks back at me, and I put enough space between us so that I can gaze into his eyes, drink him in. It's been so long, *too* long.

'What about the band?'

'I missed you. They're great guys, but… I like it when it's us.'

I throw my arms around his neck and pull him close to me. He buries his face in my hair. I close my eyes and we hold on to each other as if we never want to let go.

I trace my finger over his jawline and kiss him slowly on the lips. 'I missed you too.'

He reaches for my hand and places my palm on his shirt, just over his heart.

'I had the test.'

Tears begin to well in my eyes. Is that why he's here? To tell me that he's only got a short time left? My hand flies to my mouth and I hear myself gasp and whimper. I need to sit down; if he says what I think he is going say, I'm going need to lie down, flat down on the dirt beneath me until it swallows me up. Right now, at this moment, I actually understand fully for the first time Danny's fear. Because I am afraid of what's going to come out of his mouth next. Actually, if I had a choice, I think I'd ask him not to tell me; I'd rather live in blissful ignorance, because finding out the truth is too big a risk. I hate myself for encouraging him to get checked out; what on earth was I thinking? Of course not knowing is better than receiving this kind of news…

'Danny, I was wrong, so wrong and out of order, and I'm so sorry, I am so so sorry…'

He draws me close, then trails his lips up to my ear. 'It's okay,' he whispers. 'I'm clear. Heart of an ox. Not going anywhere for a long time.'

I move my hand to the back of his neck, pulling him to me with such urgency that I can feel the beating of his heart against mine, and I'm instantly aware that they are perfectly in sync.

He lifts a stray tendril from my cheek and loops it around my ear. 'So thank you. I thought long and hard about what you said. And you were right. I was scared. Scared to die but also scared to live. And I realised that even if it was bad news, I'd be able to get through it if we were together. So can we?'

'Can we what?' I whisper, relief flooding through me. He's here. And he's okay. God, those words are precious. In this instant, I know how much he means to me, how much I want him with me always.

'Can we be together? Tell me we can. Because that's what I want do with my life: spend it loving you. Evelyn, I love you. I love you so much. I love everything about you. That you took a chance on me and that you understand me and that despite everything we've been through, you believed in me, no matter how much it hurt you. I love your courage and your selflessness, and most of all, I love that I'm the only one who gets to love all these things about you.'

I laugh, bowing my head towards my tummy.

'Not for long.' I take both his hands and place them either side of my belly button. 'We've got company, Danny.'

He blinks, staring down at his splayed hands and then back up at me, a spark of realisation dancing in his eyes.

'You can't mean…?'

I nod. 'Danny Foy, we're having a baby. We're having *our* baby.'

He drops to his knees, wraps his arms around my legs and presses his ear against my stomach. I can tell by the slight shudder in his shoulders that he is crying. And he's not the only one. I wipe away the tears streaming from my own eyes. We've found it, we've made it. We are our forever family. It came true. It's happened. It's happening for us, for now and for always.

He kisses me over and over and over.

He's a part of me now. And I'm a part of him. And this baby is part of us.

And neither of us has ever felt so much, so deeply, so suddenly all at once.

We never dreamt there was so much to feel.

CHAPTER THIRTY-ONE

It is the day of the auction. I don't know why Danny and I are dressed in our Sunday best, but we are. It's not like they care about anything other than our money, but still, we are the first people here as we want to get the best seats, scout out the competition and make sure we are in with a fighting chance of walking away today as the highest bidders and the new owners of Rosie Munroe's. We know it's a long shot, but we also know that it's worth shooting for the stars, because sometimes they may be closer than they appear.

Ruby is going to call in to say hello. Christy's coming along also with some of the old regulars for moral support and probably just a bit of a nosy. It will be nice to catch up with everyone, and win or lose we'll go for a drink and a bite to eat afterwards, and that will be worth the trip to Dublin from Ballybeg in itself.

We sit together in the back row, so that way we have a full view of everything, especially any potential competition that might try to bid against us. Danny squeezes my hand. It's as clammy and sweaty as his.

'What are you thinking?' I ask him.

He blows out his cheeks. 'I think we've got a great chance. The reserve is two hundred thousand, so considerably less than Christy estimated. We've got two hundred and forty between us, so even if someone tries to outbid us right from the start, we've got some wriggle room. We could scare them off quickly when they realise that we're prepared to raise the stakes.'

I smile at him and curl my lip, 'Big stakes, eh?'

He nods, and clenches his fists. I know he wants this just as much as I do. And now that we've got junior to think of, and Danny is planning for a life beyond tomorrow, our timing could not be more perfect.

Rosie Munroe's, we love you. Just let us win. We'll give you our forever, I promise.

Moments before the auction is set to start, the room starts to fill up. Serious-looking men in dark suits – developers, I'd say – stand around the sides of the room, phones in one hand and calculators in the other. Farmers in holey knitted jumpers shuffle into the rows as if they're coming late to Saturday-night mass. A distinguished-looking woman in a fitted jacket with designer glasses perched on the end of her nose sits keying details into an iPad and taking photos of the updated catalogue.

I dip my eyes and reread the spec, trying to convince myself that none of these people are here for Rosie Munroe's. What would that farmer want with a pub in the city? No, surely they must be here for the other stuff. Danny and I are here; we've got the cash. My perfect scenario would play out like this: the image of Rosie Munroe's flashes up on the big screen, the room stays still and silent. I raise my paddle high over my head, nobody budges and the auctioneer gives me the thumbs-up just before he smashes the hammer down on the block and shouts, 'Going, going, gone to the lady in the blue dress at the back. Next lot, please.'

Then we collect the keys and a beautiful new life begins. For all of us.

When I explained to Mum what we were doing, she said that she'd asked for some advice around the village and learnt that sometimes the bank is willing to take lower than the reserve just to cover the majority of the debt and cut their losses. So her advice was not even to bid straight away; to wait and see. She added that they might even lower the price. 'You could walk out of there with the pub and a nice bit of cash left over if you play it smart.'

I thanked her, but there is no way I'd gamble that way. That strategy is too high-risk for us. We don't want just any pub; we want Rosie's, and we don't care if it costs us our last cent if it means we win. So before the auctioneer even utters the words, I'm going to wave my paddle high above my head like an air-traffic controller.

A hush descends, and a tubby, red-faced gentleman dressed in a three-piece beige suit, with a toupee that looks like a squirrel's tail, walks out onto the stage. He takes his place at the stand and raises his hammer.

'Good afternoon, ladies and gentlemen. We have an exciting catalogue in house for you today. There's been lots of speculative interest from overseas, so keep your hats on: this could be a tense experience for some of you. Without further ado, we'll begin. Lot One: an eight-bedroom guest house on the Malahide Road, extensive gardens and period features. Ready for immediate occupancy with no major refurbishment required. We'll start with the reserve price of one hundred and fifty thousand. Any bids at one fifty?'

He scans the room. I sit on my paddle. I'm delighted that we took seats in the back row. It would kill me to sit at the front and not know what was going on.

Not one paddle is raised in the air for the guest house.

Danny elbows me gently and gives me a wink. This is looking favourable for us. Perhaps all that overseas interest was just a ruse to put people on edge. I have to say, it nearly worked on me.

The auctioneer squints around one last time and returns to the paper in his hand. 'We have instructions to lower the reserve in the case of no bidders. So let's start at one twenty; any buyers at one hundred and twenty thousand? A fine property, tremendous amount of commercial potential or indeed a splendid family home, a stone's throw from pubs, restaurants, parks and theatres.'

I'm starting to think my mother was on to something. Maybe there is a strategy amongst this motley crew.

But still not one single paddle. If anything, people seem to be keeping their heads down, avoiding eye contact altogether.

The auctioneer looks to the side of the stage, where four men dressed in suits sit, laptop and phone in front of each of them. 'Online bids? Phone bids?' he asks, but they all shake their heads solemnly.

I'd not really thought about overseas or remote competition in this regard. Who'd be tuned into an Irish auction in Texas or Mozambique or Japan? Why on earth would someone phone up to buy something they can't be bothered to show up and view in person? What an easy job those men must have, sitting there not answering phones or receiving online bids all day.

I lean over to Danny and whisper in his ear. 'I think this is a really good sign. That house is amazing, and much cheaper than Rosie Munroe's. If they don't like that, they are going to run a mile from an inner-city pub that's nowhere near as posh and twice the price!'

We sit through the next few lots and everything goes at reserve price to the first and only bidder.

Perfect. Soon Danny and I will waltz out of here with the papers to say we're back in business.

And then it is the turn of Lot Five. This is us. We shuffle up in our seats, trying not to look too keen but wanting to be in the best possible listening position.

'Iconic inner-city pub north of the river, has undergone some recent renovations and substantial investment; music, food and drinks licence, potential for accommodation upstairs, parking at rear. Sold as a going concern. Let's start at the reserve price of two hundred thousand euros.'

And before I even get to raise my paddle in the air, they are off.

'Two hundred thousand to the gentleman on the left. Can I get two ten, anyone for two ten?'

I lift my paddle, but someone in the front has beaten me to it.

'Lady in the front, two ten; do I hear two twenty?'

This is war. I stand up with my paddle and swing it from side to side as high as I can. Danny is ready to wolf-whistle if the auctioneer misses me.

'Lady at the back in the blue dress, two twenty; does anyone want to go higher than two twenty?'

I'm muttering, 'Don't you dare, fuckers,' but they do – they want to go higher.

'Back to the man on my left, two thirty. Anyone for two forty?'

He's jumping ten grand as if we were playing with Monopoly money. This is a HUGE sum of real-life money; a huge sum of blood, sweat and tears. Especially tears! I glance at Danny; this is our whole pot. He nods, and I wave my paddle frantically.

'Lady in blue at the back, two forty. Anyone for two fifty?'

There's a lull. I risk taking a breath, and Danny slides his hand around my waist. It's a stretch, but I think we've done it.

'Two forty, anyone higher than two forty?' The auctioneer raises his hammer. 'Two hundred and forty thousand, going once…'

The suited man is back, I glance over at him, his phone tucked into his neck. He raises his finger.

'Two forty-five? We've got two forty-five…'

What a bastard.

I drop my paddle to the floor. Two hundred and forty-five thousand is too much. Anything over two forty we simply haven't got.

I flop into my seat, disappointment coursing through my body. I take out my phone and text my mum and Tara. *No good. Gone to 245* 😟

Mr Suited Developer has put his phone away now. He scans the room, confident that he's closed the deal. The auctioneer raises his hammer.

Danny strokes my back. 'It's okay, we'll find something else, don't worry.'

There's a tap on my shoulder, and then I feel a soft cupped hand curl around my ear.

'Go another ten, Evelyn.'

I turn around. It's Liz. Silver-haired Liz from the pub.

'I owe you,' she says. 'You've given me some great tips.'

I'm breathless, I can't process this fast enough. But another ten puts us back in the game. Maybe I could pay her back…

'Going, going…'

Liz snatches my paddle from under my seat and raises it high in the air with a haughty nod.

'Two fifty from the silver-haired lady at the back!'

I turn around. What on earth is she doing? But I don't have time to thank her.

The developer won't be outdone. He raises his finger. 'We have two fifty-five, thank you, sir.'

Danny shakes his head.

'Any advance on two fifty-five?'

My paddle is snatched from me a second time.

'Two sixty from the distinguished gentleman at the back, thank you, sir.'

Before I can even turn my head, I hear Danny crying, 'Christy, you legend!'

We are WINNING!

'Looking to close now, folks, any last bids? Last chance. Any takers? Rosie Munroe's at two hundred and sixty thousand euros. Going once… going twice…'

But then suddenly a hand shoots forward from the table at the side. One of the men sitting at the laptops is nodding, his eyes set on the auctioneer.

'Internet bid at two sixty-five.'

And we are out. Again.

Nobody snatches my paddle now. I look around to Liz and Christy, their sorry, pinched expressions telling me there's nothing left in the pot. I sit back to watch the last act of this theatre, watch the devastation of our dream play out till the end.

'Gentleman on the left, have I got two seventy for one of the oldest pubs in the heart of Dublin, home to many a literary and musical icon… Have I got two hundred and seventy thousand euros?'

Mr Developer takes the phone from his ear and shakes his head. He's out too.

'Any more takers for Rosie Munroe's?' Everyone in the room is swivelling around now, wondering if anyone else is going to swoop in at the last minute.

I pick up my bag and check my phone, anything to distract myself from this slow torture. A text message from Mum. I imagine it will be full of commiserations, lit candles and prayers to the patron saint of last-minute miracles. I click it open.

I have 20k to add. Stick up that paddle and let's bring this baby home!

'Lot Five. Rosie Munroe's at two hundred and sixty-five thousand euros. Going once, going twice…'

'Wait! We have it!' I leap out of my chair and beat my paddle against the air. 'Two seventy, we have it!'

Danny looks up at me in complete confusion. But I give him a little wink, and then my dream scenario plays out just as I imagined. The room stays still and silent. I keep my paddle high over my head, nobody budges, and the auctioneer gives me the thumbs-up just before he smashes the hammer down on the block and shouts, '*Gone* to the lady in the blue dress at the back. Next lot, please.'

And we collect the keys and a beautiful new life begins.

For all of us.

EPILOGUE

I am huge.

I stand, back arched, hands on my hips, filling the doorway of Rosie Munroe's. The first buds of spring have started to push through the soil in our little raised flower beds. A gentle breeze stirs the cherry blossom trees that line the street, showering us with pink and white petals like confetti. In the sky directly above, I watch a green-emblazoned plane make its descent. That'll be Tara, arriving in plenty of time for my 'surprise' birthday party tomorrow. Liz let it slip when she asked if she could bring anything. I've sworn to look suitably overcome. To be honest, that comes easy to me these days. I am overcome with gratitude and love and elation all the time. And frequently with hunger, too, particularly for peanut butter and crisp sandwiches.

I hear Mum's laugh inside as she sits and chats with Christy at the bar over a fresh pot of tea. They get on like a house on fire; she loves hearing his stories and he seems very taken with her also. We held a traditional folk night here on Sunday, a proper ceilidh, and the two of them jigged and reeled until the early hours. It was so busy and well received that we've decided to add it regularly to the calendar, try to make room for it somewhere in between all the live gigs and open-mic nights we've got lined up.

I smile and pat my hands against my thighs as Muffin pounds down the street towards me. Martin follows him, the lead looped in his hand. Once Muffin reaches me, she brushes up against my leg and then nuzzles into the bowl of dog biscuits we keep under the picnic tables.

'Glorious day,' Martin says. 'I'll make use of the fine weather and try to build that sand box now, if that suits?'

I nod my agreement. 'You're a star,' I tell him as he heads inside to climb the back stairs to the roof garden, where he lives in an amazing little wooden pod that he built himself. He's our doorman and carpenter, our dog-walker, painter, decorator, sound man, back-up barman and general life-saver. After we signed on the dotted line at the auction house and Danny and I started drawing up our plans and thinking about staff, Martin was the first person I thought of. We found him still wrapped in blankets and cardboard by the bus stop. I explained to him that Rosie Munroe's had given me more than a job and a home; it had given me a life and a family. And if he was interested, I'd love him to join us. He did, and now he is part of our little tribe, our life and our family.

A few weeks after we took over Rosie's, Danny and I had to go for the first baby scan at the hospital. Danny was white with nerves. We waited patiently in the sticky plastic seating until our names were called by the sonographer. I stretched out on the chair and raised my T-shirt to offer up my bulging belly. She smeared cool clear jelly over it and began to navigate what looked like a moonscape on a little ultrasound screen to our left. I answered all her questions and made light chit-chat. All went well until her brow furrowed and a tense hush fell on all three of us. She adjusted her earpiece, pursing her lips in puzzlement.

Something isn't right, I thought. And I feared the worst. Was she straining to hear a heartbeat? An infinitesimal shift in the tilt of her head sent a surge of panic through me; Danny too. His face was now grey. We looked at each other... Something was definitely wrong.

But then she nodded to herself and a smile broke her lips. 'Two heartbeats.' She lifted her head. 'Congratulations, you've got two babies in there.'

It took a long slow-motion moment for it to register. Nothing was wrong. Everything was fine. Everything was beyond fine; it was terrific. It was more than I'd ever dared to dream. I glanced from Danny to the screen, to my slimy tummy, back to the sonographer. She pointed a finger to two tiny white bean-shapes, one couched on top of the other, like they were in monochrome bunk beds.

'Are there twins in the family?' she asked, and I looked to Danny.

His face flushed and he laughed, rubbing his eyes 'Yes. Yes, there are.'

That was a few months back. We've been getting ready for their arrival ever since.

I say hello to customers old and new as I waddle across the pub floor and climb the stairs to the living space we've refurbished on the first and second floors. In the big airy nursery, newly painted and gleaming white, Danny is measuring and marking up as he hangs a shelf. I need to catch my breath each time I walk in, my eyes swelling with grateful tears when I see the two hand-built cribs waiting patiently for next month. He dusts off his hands. 'Any idea what you want to put up there?'

'Yep, I know just the thing,' I say.

Yesterday, the postman delivered a padded envelope. Inside was a postcard-size watercolour from Ruby: a beautiful aerial view of a little town where tall trees and wild flowers grow freely. A winding river circles this nameless place, protecting its rows of dainty houses painted in bright, deep colours, all lined up like misfit dominoes of red and yellow and blue. A term into art college, thanks to her successful bursary application, she's moved on from drawing faces with leftover make-up and has a palette full of new colours, new techniques, new visions. Her world has opened up.

Danny places the little painting on the shelf, admiring how its hints of gold and silver glimmer in the afternoon sun.

Without warning, I double over and hold my tummy, overwhelmed by a sudden rumble of kicking. He catches me anxiously by the elbows.

'Are you all right? Are they at it again?'

'I think they're trying to break out!'

I slide down the wall and try to steady the toss and tumble of our unborn babies as they spin and surge inside me. And I realise that it's here. That I'm not on the outside of my life any more. I'm in it, living it. I am the woman I dreamt of being. Here, like déjà vu, is the snapshot of my vision, of a forever home and a forever family, a dream that I kept faithfully folded up in a deep crease in my heart for so very long. If there's one thing I have learnt on this journey, it's that having faith means trusting in advance what only makes sense in reverse.

And that every dream begins with a dreamer. And every dreamer begins with a dream.

I used to tip my head skywards and wish for more, for better, for different. Sometimes it all seems so impossibly far, too impossibly hard. But that glimmer in the distance, that sparkle in the sky, is within our grasp if we trust our own light to help us steer our course and remember never to fear the darkness. Because it's in the darkness that we can find ourselves shining most brightly.

Danny kneels down and presses his ear against my navel. A smile creeps across his lips as he starts to sing, and the kicking subsides.

We are almost there, and nowhere near. We set our sights and it's brought us here. We are exactly as we are meant to be, with all the infinite possibilities born of hope.

And there is nothing beyond our reach.

A LETTER FROM COLLEEN

I want to say a huge thank you for choosing to read *I'm Still Standing*. If you did enjoy it, and want to keep up to date with all my latest releases, just sign up at the following link. Your email address will never be shared and you can unsubscribe at any time.

www.bookouture.com/colleen-coleman/?title=im-still-standing

I hope you loved *I'm Still Standing*; if you did, I would be very grateful if you could write a review. I'd love to hear what you think, and it makes such a difference helping new readers to discover my books for the first time.

I love hearing from my readers – you can get in touch on my Facebook page or through Twitter.

I have thoroughly enjoyed writing about Evelyn and discovering her journey with her. Creating a story set in Ireland with a full cast of Irish characters has been wonderful, as it is my home; a beautiful, rich and diverse country with so much to offer, from the wild Atlantic west coast to the cosmopolitan capital of Dublin. If anything, *I'm Still Standing* has made me even more homesick than usual! I really hope you enjoyed spending time with Evelyn as much as I did.

In this book, I wanted to explore our sense of place, personal and geographical, and how our identity is linked with that. Homelessness is not just losing the roof over your head, but can often feel like losing your place in the world. A donation from the sales of *I'm Still Standing* will be given to supporting homelessness charities across our cities. So by simply buying this book, you have helped someone, somewhere receive a little relief, a little comfort, and a little nudge to say that their welfare matters to us, so thank you from the bottom of my heart.

Many thanks to all of you who email me, message me, chat to me on Facebook or Twitter and tell me how much you enjoy reading my books. I've been genuinely blown away by such incredible kindness and support from you all. There are so many things I love about being an author; however, my favourite has got to be this immense connection with people all over the world, from so many different walks of life, making me feel that I truly have friends everywhere.

Team Bookouture, Abigail Fenton and Emily Ruston, have made my dreams come true and encouraged me every step of the way to keep my face skyward and reach for the stars. I am indebted. I hope every next step brings you closer to where you want to be.

Thanks, happy reading and until next time,
Colleen Coleman xxx

 CollColemanAuth/

 @CollColemanAuth

BOOK DISCUSSION GUIDE

1. Evelyn had a plan but it fell apart. Do you believe that things happen for a reason or that you make your own luck?
2. A sense of place is a strong theme in this book. Does it really matter so much where you live?
3. 'I'm Still Standing' is a true feel-good, raise-your-hands-in-the-air kind of song. What's your favourite song that never fails to lift your mood?
4. Most of the characters in the book are passionate about their profession. Do you think it matters so much to your overall well-being if you love or hate your job?
5. Rosie Munroe's pub was once the social hub of the community. Do you think communities need social hubs any more?
6. 'Evelyn's mother let her own beliefs and hang-ups get in the way of her relationships.' Do you agree?
7. Evelyn is a classic Generation Y or Millennial (born between 1980 and 2000). Do you think people of her age have it harder or easier than their parents did when they were that age?
8. Which character did you most identify with? Did your opinions about any of the characters change over the course of the novel?

Now enough. That wine won't drink itself.

Coll xx

Lightning Source UK Ltd.
Milton Keynes UK
UKOW06f0713101217
314211UK00009B/389/P